THE ACCURSED

ELDRITCH AFFAIR BOOK ONE

RIAIN FOX

PROMETHEAN
— BOOKS —

Copyright © 2023 by Riain Fox

All rights reserved.

No part of this publication may be reproduced, distributed, or transmitted in any form or by any means, including photocopying, recording, or other electronic or mechanical methods, without the prior written permission of the publisher, except as permitted by U.S. copyright law. For permission requests, contact contact@prometheanbooks.com.

The story, all names, characters, and incidents portrayed in this production are fictitious. No identification with actual persons (living or deceased), places, buildings, and products is intended or should be inferred.

2nd edition

To Lynn.
Thanks for everything

Prologue

The electronic whirring fell into a mournful dirge as the stair lift neared its destination.

"Bernard?" Albert called, pitching his voice so it carried up the stairs. He paused, listening, straining his ears for a response. "If you're moping in the dark again, I'm calling Dr. Laghari and upping your meds."

"Stubborn man," he muttered.

If he would just talk to me instead of hiding in his rooms all day... He shook his head.

The chair came to a slow halt beneath him. A disdainful grimace curled his lip as he started the laborious process of levering himself onto his feet. Sharp jolts of pain prickled his feet like he'd stepped onto hot coals instead of the ancient olive shag carpet.

What's worse about getting old? All the new and constant pains or having to rely on As-Seen-On-TV contraptions to get around my own home?

As much as he hated using it, he could no longer avoid doing so. When Albert and Bernard were spry hexagenarians, Albert was filled with righteous fury over his husband's purchase. Now, even though the time it took the lift to travel was measured in geological time, Albert couldn't argue that it wasn't needed.

The muffled tapping of his cane echoed throughout the hallway. Albert turned the burnished doorknob, but the wooden door didn't budge. Grumbling curses about old wooden doors, old wooden houses, and stubborn old men, Albert set aside his cane and grabbed the knob with both hands. With a sharp squeal of protest, the door popped from the jamb and slammed against the wall.

Damn, there's another hole in the wall, Albert chided himself.

His shoulder ached where he'd given the door a little English, but he ignored the pain and reclaimed his cane. A stench wafted out of the room, Earthy and dank.

"Oh, Bernard. Again?" The frustration had seeped out of his voice, replaced instead with empathy for his husband. Albert blinked, but his rheumy eyes failed to see the details in the gloom beyond, just now realizing he'd left his glasses downstairs. "That's what the rubber sheets are for, love. No need to be embarrassed about getting older. Lord knows I've been there, too."

The floorboards groaned and creaked underfoot as he approached Albert's bed. A chill tickled his skin, setting the sparse white hairs on his arms prickling.

It was midmorning, but the drapes were still drawn. Even if he had his glasses, he probably wouldn't be able to see anything in this darkness. His footsteps kicked up dust, which set his nose to watering.

"Bernard?"

The fuzzy lump on the bed didn't respond.

THE ACCURSED

"Oh, stop being such a baby. If you just moved downstairs with me you wouldn't have had to stew in it all day. Let's just get you in the shower and we can clean all this up."

Not sharing a room. It's like we're my parents. They were old, but not *that* old. He stifled a chuckle.

As Albert drew closer to the four poster, Bernard's outline came into focus as if appearing from mist. Detailed emerged from the cataract fog, and Albert blinked, trying to make sense of it.

Bernard was in bed, uncovered and undressed. As unseasonably warm as Dunwich was this year, Albert had never known his lover to sleep without covers. He wasn't entirely naked, though. Bernard's form looked like it had sprouted thick strands of hair. For the second time in as many minutes, Albert almost laughed. Bernard started balding before his third decade, and in his eighties, he was now all but hairless.

"Bernard! What the dickens…"

The hairs—or whatever they were—covered more than just his husband. The dark paneling on the walls and the dun-colored floor had camouflaged it, but he could see it now. It coated the walls and floor like thick veins of mold. Albert's neck gave an audible crack as his gaze snapped to the floor. His house slippers were a scant six inches away from one of the mysterious dark strands. He'd have to step over it to get to the bed. His gaze snapped back to his husband, and Albert's eyes widened in horror. Whatever these things were, they weren't growing *from* Bernard…

Oh god! They're growing into *him*.

With a strangled cry, Albert surged forward with a burst of speed he'd not experienced in decades. His shins slammed into the metal bedframe, but he couldn't pay attention to his pain right then.

"Bernard!"

There was no response.

He shook his husband, but the vines held him fast. One of Albert's fingers slipped through the dense matting covering Bernard, and Albert's heart stopped.

No...He's as cold as death.

"No. No, no no no no no." Tears sprang to his eyes, occluding his already foggy vision. "Bernard, wake up. Please, wake up."

Images of their life together scrolled through his mind. The last few years hadn't exactly been good between them, but even those rocky years didn't erase the lifetime of bliss they'd had together.

Albert didn't know how long he stayed like that, weeping, until a gentle caress on the back of his hand jerked his head up.

"Bernard! Are you—"

A grasping vine slithered up his arm. He snatched his hand away and finally recognized what they were.

Roots.

Albert's hands shook as he fumbled for his cane, knocking it to the floor. Now that he wasn't weeping, he could hear a skittering sound. No, not skittering. More like the creaking of an old house during a storm as the wood swelled, contracted, and settled.

All the vines along the bed had turned toward him like the roots of a parched tree turned toward a water source during a drought. Stumbling back, Albert realized too late the roots on the floor had done the same. One pierced his house slipper, and the thing was plucked from his foot as he stumbled away.

Hundreds of wriggling tendrils waved in the air like windblown grass, all stretching toward Albert's retreating form. He searched for a clear path back to the bed. Bernard *couldn't* be gone. Not yet. Not like this.

Not without me. This isn't how it's supposed to be.

He couldn't leave him. Not alone. Not with these…things.

But the coiling strands were everywhere.

"I'm sorry." His voice cracked, and tears streamed down his cheeks, dampening the crevices of his wrinkled skin. "Please forgive me."

I'll come back for you.

Albert turned and hobbled toward the door as fast as he could, stumbling at his lopsided gait. He kicked his right foot with each step, trying to dislodge the last slipper.

The skittering tendrils covered the walls and ceiling. He'd had dreams of dying, of walking toward the glowing portal toward the afterlife. But it didn't look like this. He urged his flagging steps faster—as fast as they could go. The roots on the walls and the ceiling stretched, growing ever closer toward the door, shrinking his salvation and perverting his dream of ever after.

Albert's grunting turned into a low wail of pain, his sciatic nerve flaring in agony with each step. Before him, the roots reached the doorframe. He flung himself through the opening, his bathrobe snagging on the grasping vines.

The stair lift rested where he left it, a dozen steps away at the top of the flight.

Albert spared a glance behind him, considering his options. The deadly vines were shambling along, but so was he. If it were a straight race, Albert could win, physical ailments or not. His gaze turned to the stairway. The house was built in the 1800s. The steps were narrow and steep, with no mind given to accessibility or the frailty of the house's future owners. He didn't have time to wait for the lift. For the first time in years, Albert stepped onto the stairway.

Before his foot hit the stair, Albert knew he had made a mistake. He didn't know if his error was glancing over his shoulder as he took the first step or if it was committing to the step without having a firm hold on the banister.

Perhaps it was not checking for roots around his ankles.

He didn't have time to parse the information and figure it out.

Albert pitched forward. There was a brief moment just before the vertigo kicked in where he was weightless and gravity hadn't taken hold yet. It was almost like flying, and the sensation was both thrilling and terrifying. It was the same the first time he rode a rollercoaster. He felt it when he first lay eyes on Bernard and knew that he was destined to live a life of sin, just like his mother used to say.

Nature reasserted itself, and Albert plummeted. His mind reeled, thoughts lurching as they tried to catch up with his body's motion. Tossing his cane away so he wouldn't impale himself on it, he reached for the banister. His sweaty hand slipped from the ancient wooden rail, but his right hand slipped into the space between the banister and the wall. He braced himself as best he could and tried to arrest his fall.

The thin bones in his forearm weren't up to the task of supporting his entire weight. With a wet pop, the bones snapped. He heard it before he felt it, and he experienced a moment of almost clinical disinterest as his body fell down the stairs, and his forearm folded over parallel to itself.

Then, with a sloppy *SLURRRRRP*, his arm jerked free of the banister, and he hurtled down the stairs. He rebounded off the wall and came to rest on the landing between floors. A trail of blood marked his path.

Like a bloodhound, the roots beelined for the crimson trail, following quickly behind. Albert cradled his arm against his chest and purposely averted his eyes. If he saw the blood, he'd likely faint. He could hear the vines skittering closer, sounding like thousands of spiders as they inched along. He tried to lever himself to his knees to crawl away, but his left arm gave out, and he crashed to the staircase again.

When the first root touched his ankle, he kicked. Soon there were too many to fight. They spread across his body like he was being cocooned in a spiderweb.

Albert rolled to his back so he could look up the stairway. He never wanted to be one of those old people with regrets, who lay on their deathbed lamenting what they should have done. Even as he and Bernard aged and drifted apart, he thought there would be enough time to fix things.

"I'll see you soon," he whispered.

1

"Lord almighty, is that you, Samael Dyer?"

The words, spoken with a hint of a Southern Belle accent, greeted him as soon as he stepped foot out of his beat-up Tercel.

"Good morning, Mrs. Murray." Sam averted his eyes after sending her a quick smile, his footsteps crunching up the gravel path to Ash's front door. The step up to the porch of the idyllic two-story bungalow was a scant few paces away when she called again.

"Be a dear and fetch my paper for me, would you?" Mrs. Murray leaned against the door jamb of her own McMansion, wearing nothing but a white gossamer robe and a predatory smile. Her eyes tracked Sam as he forded the low hedge that separated the manicured lawns, tipping a large tumbler full of an orange-colored drink to her lips—her morning white sangria if Sam's memory was right.

The paperboy had done his job well, the rolled newspaper closer to the house than it was to the pristine sidewalk. Snatching it up, Sam bounded up the stairs and held it out to Ash's neighbor. She'd rested her foot on a nearby planter, and Sam fumbled the handoff when his gaze caught the expanse of flesh she was displaying.

A tanned, soft finger slid along the back of his hand as she accepted the paper.

"You turn eighteen yet, Sammy?"

"Um, yeah. A few months ago, Mrs. Murray. My birthday's the week after Mike if I remember correctly. It's hard to believe he's a freshman already."

A frown flitted across her face almost faster than Sam noticed. She took a longer pull from her drink.

"Yes, well...time has a way of slipping by. It has such a way of surprising us." She raked Sam with her gaze again. "So many...changes."

Sam cleared his throat and stepped back, stumbling on the step. Before he could make his escape, Mrs. Murray spoke.

"You still cleaning pools?" She rested the crystal tumbler against her chest, a thin bead of condensation trickling down and turning the thin white fabric nearly transparent.

Sam met Mrs. Murray's gaze, his eyes boring into hers with the effort not to look at her now-exposed nipple.

Jesus, did she practice that move? He'd be impressed if he didn't feel like a gazelle being backed into a corner by a hungry lion.

A grin parted Mrs. Murray's lips, the tips of her teeth flashing white in the thin morning light.

"No, ma'am. My mom wanted me to focus on school for this last semester."

"I thought I heard old Penny down the way mention you cleaned hers a few weeks back."

Shit. He should have known better than to try to lie. Elsbury was too small a town to get away with it. Especially with a busybody like Mrs. Murray.

THE ACCURSED

"Oh yeah, I take on a few odd jobs every now and then."

Another sip, another trickle of condensation. The round patch of dark skin was like a magnet trying to reel in Sam's attention.

"You're such a good boy helping your momma pay the bills."

"I'm not much help anymore, what with focusing on—"

She ran right over his deflection "Why don't you pencil me in this weekend? Ain't no one been able to clear my filter out proper since you were here last summer."

A silent war raged inside Sam. On one hand, there was a reason he stopped servicing the Murrays' pool. He couldn't deny that Mrs. Murray was smokin' hot. She may be his mother's age, but she had kept it tight. Unfortunately, cougars weren't really his thing. Especially when they were married, the mother of a younger classmate, and lived next door to his neighbor. On the other hand...

We could really use the money.

Resigning himself to a day of being eye-fucked by the cougar, Sam nodded.

"Yes, ma'am. How about Saturday?"

She showed a little more teeth. "Atta boy, Sammy. Mr. Murray is playing golf with the judge that afternoon, and I would hate to disturb his morning routine. Best to come by after he leaves."

Sam nodded and finally made it off the porch.

"It's supposed to be hot this weekend, so make sure you dress appropriately."

His neck felt like rubber as he nodded mutely, trying to keep his smile from turning into a grimace.

"Oh, and make sure you bring that brush of yours, the one on that long, hard pole. The last pool boy had a pitifully short one, and just wasn't able to...reach all my nooks and crannies."

"I'll...bring my longest," he said through a plastered-on smile.

"Oh I know you will, Sammy."

As soon as she waved, Sam booked it, practically running as soon as he cleared the hedge, and he didn't stop until he was through the Williams' front door.

"Mornin'," Mr. Williams said as Sam stepped into the kitchen. Mr. Williams sat at the kitchen table, taking absent bites of his breakfast while reading the paper. A large mug of coffee steamed in front of him. Black, and no doubt piping hot just the way he and his daughter liked it. He was a big man. Not fat, but he took up *a lot* of space. Sam often joked that Mr. Williams should have been in the Marines, but despite his size, Mr. Williams was far too gentle a soul for the military.

Barkley, the Williams' puppy Bassett, came barreling around the corner. The tile proved too slick for his overlarge paws, and the pup scrabbled for a few moments before he got enough friction built up to pounce on Sam.

Sam bent down and scruffled the pup's head and tugged on its huge ears. "Who's a good boy? Who's the best boy?"

Barkley quickly lost interest in Sam and went careening out of the kitchen the same way he came in.

"Anything new in the world?" Sam asked, pulling out a chair and sitting for what he knew would be a long wait.

THE ACCURSED

Mr. Williams grunted. Polite he may be, but he was a man of few words, especially while reading. After a moment, he folded the paper up and tossed it on the table. He was wearing what he called his "dirty work" clothes. He'd been a plumber longer than Sam had been alive, so Sam didn't want to think about what Mr. Williams considered a *dirty* job. Over the work outfit was a tiny red-and-white apron that read *World's Okayest Chef*.

"More trouble over at MU," he said after swallowing a bite of breakfast. He wiped at the crumbs clinging to his prodigious chin and shook his head. "It's always something with that place."

"What's it this time?" Sam almost didn't ask. Mr. Williams may have been a man of few words, but he *loved* to gossip about the university.

"More malarkey with a rights advocacy group. Probably didn't get the right permits to do experiments on monkeys." He shook his head again and let out a long breath through his nose. "Did I ever tell you about the time I worked on the pipes in the admin building?"

Luckily, Sam didn't have to sit through another rendition of the tale—and the accompanying conspiracy theories. Ash chose that moment to come bouncing down the stairs.

"Mornin', Pops." She gave the big man a kiss on his cheek. "Hey, Sam," she said, breezing by him and filling a travel mug full of coffee. Sam shuddered at the bitter scent of the brew. No doubt it was strong enough to dissolve nails.

"Mornin', pumpkin. You're down early," Mr. Williams said with a sly look toward Sam. The two share a silent grin. Ash's inability to get anywhere on time was the stuff of legend.

She rolled her eyes while taking a long sip, the drink so hot it would've melted Sam's face off. "*Someone* had to save Sam from yet another retelling of your terrifying trek through the bowels of the university."

"Have I told you that story before?"

Sam shrugged, but Ash wasn't so politic.

"Only like a *million times*, Dad."

Mr. Williams sent Sam a questioning glance.

"Um, maybe not quite that many times..."

"Don't listen to him. He's too polite to say otherwise."

Sam smiled sheepishly.

"You should have said something, Sammy."

"Sorry, Mr. Williams."

"Don't apologize. It's just that if you don't speak up, you'll—" Mr. Williams did a double-take, and his eyes bugged out. "Ashley, put some clothes on! We have company." He said the last in a strained whisper like Sam wasn't a scant few feet away.

Ash waved an absent hand. "Sam hardly counts as company. Besides, it's not like he hasn't seen me naked." She strutted around the kitchen table, shaking her hips and shoulders in an awkward pantomime of a dance, sporting nothing but a worn T-shirt and undies.

She was right, of course. Sam *had* seen her in much less, and many times. He hadn't even noticed what she was wearing until her dad said something. Compared to some of Ash's other outfits, her pajamas didn't even rate on the scandalous scale. Sam had spent many summers in the Williams' swimming pool. Compared to her swimwear, Ash's pajamas were practically a nun's habit. Hell, like she said, they'd seen each other naked tons of times.

THE ACCURSED

Mr. Williams spluttered. "You were just kids. That's different and you know it."

"We're still kids."

"Eighteen isn't a kid," he growled, scowling at his grinning daughter.

"Does that mean you'll let me take the car?"

Those words took Mr. Williams by surprise, and he shut his mouth with an audible click. Sam tried to hide his grin. Ash may have been an adult, but Mr. Williams still didn't think she was ready to drive. Sam couldn't disagree. She was unpredictable enough without being behind the wheel of a one-ton mobile weapon.

Mr. Williams shook his head in defeat. "Just go get ready."

Ash laughed at her father's dejected expression and headed back upstairs, calling over her shoulder, "Don't worry, Pop. I won't dress like this when Randy comes to pick me up." Distant thumps and bangs sounded as Hurricane Ashley swept through her bedroom and bathroom.

Mr. Williams massive shoulders slumped in defeat. He cast a commiserating glance at Sam. "Don't worry, Sammy. She won't be with that"—his jaw worked like he was trying to chew rocks—"*boy* for much longer."

Sam's spine jerked straight, and a sheen of sweat coated his palms. "Um, I don't know what you mean."

"Sure ya don't, Sammy." The older man chuckled and leaned forward like he was sharing a secret. "I know it's hard to believe right now because you're still kids, but this Randy character won't be around for long. Maybe tomorrow or months from now, but eventually, she'll see what's in front of her."

A yawning hole opened in Sam's stomach, and he had to swallow a few times before he could speak. "I don't— It's not like..." He closed his eyes and took a breath. "We're just friends, Mr. W."

"Ayeup," he agreed with a smirk. "Trust me. That's exactly what happened with me and Aman—" his voice cut off.

Shit, he thought. *Say something quick!*

The yawning hole in Sam's stomach swallowed the entire room. The silence was as thick in the air as the smell of bacon and eggs. Unlike Ash, Sam didn't have a knack for filling every beat of silence with chatter, so the two just sat in awkward silence.

After a moment, Mr. Williams cleared his throat. "How's the school year coming along? Grades still good?" He didn't give Sam a chance to answer before throwing his hands in the air. "Course they are! Who am I talking to here?"

Sam bobbed his head from side to side. Mr. Williams wasn't wrong. Sam was so keyed up about his grades that he was weeks ahead in all his coursework.

"What about college? Get all your apps in?"

"Yes, sir. I submitted them all last November."

"Good on you. I wish I knew Ashley's plans. I'd ask you, but you're probably just as clueless."

Sam nodded. Unlike him, Ash wasn't much of a planner. He'd known since the third grade which college he wanted to attend. Of course, that didn't stop him from submitting applications to nine other universities. He would've submitted more, but he couldn't afford the application fees.

"Still hoping for MU?"

"Yes, sir."

THE ACCURSED

Mr. Williams held the university in high suspicion, but he acknowledged it was still a top-tier school. That, and its generous grant program for locals made it Sam's first choice.

"Well, they don't take slackers, so keep it up. I know I speak for Alice when I say that we're proud of what you've accomplished so far."

"Thanks, Mr. Williams," Sam said through an unexpected lump in his throat. Ever since Sam's dad left, Mr. Williams had basically become his surrogate father.

"For the love of Pete, Sam. Call me Bruce."

"You know that's never gonna happen, Pops," Ash said, reappearing in the kitchen.

Sam jumped. Ash was wearing something Mr. Williams would approve of—well, something he'd disapprove less of. The sight of her turned that yawning pit in his stomach into a vortex, and his hands went clammy again.

Did she hear what Mr. Williams said?

She gave him an odd look. "Ready to go? I've been waiting hours for you two to stop gabbing."

2

THE AIR WAS CHILLY but not overly so. The frigid claws of winter didn't normally let up until well into April, but this year, Spring hadn't crept into Elsbury as much as knocked its door down with a wrecking ball. If today held like the week previous, he'd discard his light flannel by third period.

Unfortunately, his beat-up Tercel was still in the driveway. Despite leaving it unlocked, no one had deigned to steal it. Ash said its "urban camouflage" kept it safe; the Frankencar's body was cobbled together by no fewer than four other Tercels. Of course, none of them were the same forest green as the original, so the old Toyota looked like it had been dressed by a manic toddler.

Sam headed for the passenger door while Ash slipped into the driver's seat. Despite Mr. Williams' hesitation about his daughter's ability to drive, she usually drove them to school. Of course, that didn't mean she was any good at it.

"What's that?" she asked, nodding toward the back seat.

"Oh right. It's from Mom. She thought you'd like it."

Ash surveyed the garment over her shoulder and nodded. She cranked the starter, and the Tercel roared to life on the first try, squealing in protest when she left the ignition turned a little too long. Sam winced but wisely kept his mouth shut.

Before she could throw the car into reverse, Sam slammed the seatbelt in place. "What's for breakfast?"

"Is that a rhetorical question?"

Sam rolled his eyes, knowing full well that Ash craved a McMuffin every morning like a drowning man who longed for land.

As they pulled out of the driveway, Mrs. Murray came into view, lounging on the wicker bench on her porch, her head tilted back and her chest thrusting out.

Ash made a noise in the back of her throat. "She try getting in your pants again?"

Sam ripped his gaze away and back toward the road ahead. "That's a big 10-4. I um...I'll be cleaning their pool this weekend."

She snorted and aimed the car toward downtown. "You gonna wear those shorts she likes so much?"

"Ugh, please don't remind me."

"You know, you don't *have* to go over."

Sam's head slammed into the headrest as the car accelerated like they were starting the Indy 500 instead of driving through the suburbs. "We could use the money."

Ash snorted again. "And this way you don't have to say no." She laughed when she saw Sam's expression. "You know you don't have to wear the shorts, right?"

"Last time I didn't she 'accidentally' spilled a pitcher of sweet tea on me. She gave me a pair of Mike's shorts to wear."

"He's like half your size."

"I think that was the point," he deadpanned, trying not to take her cackling laughter personally.

Working for Mrs. Murray was a pain and a little uncomfortable—well, *really* uncomfortable—but while she made her interest obvious, she was harmless. And what he told Ash was true. He and his mom could really use the money, so he'd endure an afternoon of being leered at, and yes, he would wear the tight swim trunks. He'd at least get a good tip out of it.

It's no different than waitresses dressing up and flirting with customers to get better tips, right?

Sam's face burned, and he wanted to change the subject away from the neighbor's odd behavior.

"Are you ready for the Econ test today?"

They were already out of the suburbs. The modern houses and manicured lawns gave way to...houses that looked more lived in. Not rundown, but these weren't places that hired professional landscapers. Sam and his mom lived on the far side of this neighborhood. If there was an "other side of the tracks" in Elsbury, this was it. Though there weren't any tracks in Elsbury. The town was so far off the beaten path that the local joke was the only way people found the place was by taking the wrong fork on the way to the larger and much better-known Dunwich. Not that Dunwich was that much larger than Elsbury, but it had the advantage of being just off the highway.

Ash cursed and took the right onto Main Street too tight, even for her. Luckily, the stop sign on the corner was far enough back that the car missed it. The original sign hadn't been so lucky, having been taken out by an inattentive driver one morning last August, and the city wisely put the replacement in a safer location. As the tires rubbed against the curb, Sam was grateful for the new placement. Duct tape, baling wire, and hopes held his Tercel together. It couldn't take many more encounters with traffic signs.

The car dipped as it rolled off the curb again. "Shit! I completely forgot about the test. I was out late with Randy."

"It's open notes."

"That would be great if I *had* notes." She cast a sly look at him. "I don't suppose you…"

Sam pulled a thin stack of papers from his backpack and tossed it on her lap. She looked down briefly—garnering a honk of protest from another driver when the front of the Tercel breached the double yellow—and grinned.

"Who wrote these?" It was obvious the pink, loopy handwriting wasn't Sam's.

"I gave Janiece five bucks to copy mine."

"It's a little weird you get your 11-year-old neighbor to help you cheat." But she was smiling when she said it.

"First, she's twelve—"

"That's not any better."

"Second, she's not helping me cheat. She's helping *you* cheat."

"Thank the gods for amoral preteens."

"Third, you're welcome."

"You're the best. Have I told you that lately?"

"Not recently, and never often enough."

Ash pulled into the McDonald's parking lot and gunned it—as much as a '93 Tercel could be gunned—to beat another car to the drive thru. The driver honked, and Ash gave him a one-fingered salute in reply. Sam slunk down in his seat to avoid the angry glare reflecting from the side mirror. With a crackle of static, the speaker on the menu came alive. Ash placed the order for both of them, eliciting a groan from Sam.

"Oh, suck it up, buttercup. One McMuffin won't ruin your shapely figure."

"You say that every day."

"And I'm right every day."

"Only because I work twice as hard to compensate for the calories."

"*Delicious* calories," she whispered, pulling forward to within inches of the car in front of them.

"If you say so." As much as he complained about Ash's bad influence on his strict diet, he couldn't deny his love for the sausage and biscuit breakfast sandwich.

"Consider it repayment for the notes."

"You don't have to repay me."

"Oh, but I *insist*."

"I don't think it counts as repayment if you were going to order it for me anyways."

"McMuffin isn't good enough for you? I could get you something else."

"Please don't."

"Oh, I know!" she said, talking over him and practically bouncing in her seat. "I could put in a good word for you with Veronica. What, are you back to pretending like you haven't had a hard-on for her since the eighth grade?"

"It has *not* been since eighth grade."

Ash barked a laugh and pulled forward to the second window. The small window rattled open, and before the employee could open her mouth to greet them, Ash nearly poked her in the face with an outstretched credit card, her attention and eyes still on Sam.

"You're a damned liar, Samael Dyer. You've had a boner for Veronica Chambers since the eighth-grade pool party when her top came off and you saw her boobs."

Sam opened his mouth to protest, and she cut him off with a raised finger. He decided it wasn't worth the argument. "Fine. Just lower your voice." He hunkered down farther in his seat.

"Trust me, I would know. I had to listen to you talk about her boobs *all summer long*. And I get it, she's stacked. But I couldn't even mention going swimming without you scampering off to the bathroom to take care of business."

"Oh, god, please kill me now."

"Here's your card..." The girl at the window held it out, casting a side-eye glance at Sam.

"Thanks so much!" Ash took it and the bag that followed. Passing the bag off to Sam, Ash slid the car away from the window. He riffled through it with practiced efficiency and groaned.

"What'd they mess up this time?" Ash guessed.

"Mine. But it's fine. I'll just—" The seatbelt slamming into his chest cut the words off, and he had to scramble to keep the bag of greasy food from rocketing out of his lap.

"What's the point in ordering"—the transmission groaned in protest as she threw the car into reverse—"if they're just gonna give you whatever the hell they want."

"Seriously, Ash, it's fine. I'll just eat it."

The tip of her tongue stuck out as she reversed through the drive-thru. Sam fumbled for the 'Oh Shit' handle. Reversing was Ash's nemesis. It was in her top five most difficult driving maneuvers along with gentle left turns, traffic lights, on-ramps, and stop signs.

"The line has already moved forward," he protested, his voice rising as the Tercel whipped around the turn. The driver behind them slammed on his brakes when he noticed the Tercel's patchwork back-end careening toward him. His horn blared.

"Blow it out your ass, grandpa!" Thankfully, Ash didn't plow into the car, instead inching farther and farther back with clear intent. She widened her eyes at the other driver to let him know she meant business. It took thirty seconds of honking and angry cursing before the driver realized it'd just be faster to do what Ash wanted—a lesson six-year-old Sam learned a long time ago.

The employee was leaning through the window in confusion when Ash pulled up for the second time, this time in reverse. Ash waved the McMuffin at her. "This isn't what he ordered."

The girl threw a dirty glance at Sam. "Most people just come inside if their order is wrong."

"That would defeat the purpose of using the *drive thru.*" Ash spoke like she was explaining something to a particularly dim child.

Sam slouched in his seat again.

The girl grabbed the abomination from Ash and disappeared into the restaurant. Ash unbuckled and leaned out of the window to peer into the restaurant.

"What are you doing?" he asked.

"Making sure they don't spit in your McMuffin."

Sam shook his head. He should have known better than to let on that his order was wrong.

"Yeah, I'm watching you. Shouldn't you have a hair net on?"

Ten minutes later, they bumped into a parking spot at the high school.

Sam fought to keep his orange juice from sloshing out of its cup. "Congratulations. I give it a six."

"Out of ten?"

"Out of a hundred." Sam laughed when the bright smile on Ash's face melted.

"Asshole." She unbuckled and pulled the visor down to glance in the mirror. "We're still in one piece."

"Small miracles..." Sam muttered.

The roof rang out as Ash snapped the visor closed. "I heard that." She twisted and grabbed the shirt his mom sent for her. Throwing it over the steering wheel, she pulled off her own shirt, a pink bra the only thing separating her from a charge of indecent exposure.

This wasn't the first time Sam had seen Ash in her undies—they'd been best friends since they were five and had been inseparable ever since—but for some reason, Sam's face burned at the sight, and he turned away.

Damn it, Mr. Williams. Why'd you have to stir things up?

"Jesus, Ash. What if a teacher sees you?"

"They'd be so lucky."

A group of their classmates chose that moment to walk by. One guy spotted Ash and elbowed another. Their mouths and eyes opened to ridiculous sizes, and one of them gave Sam a double thumbs-up. Sam gave them a pained smile, and the guys moved off before Ash pulled her head through the new shirt.

"Oh. My. *Gawd*. Ashley Williams, are you so desperate that you're letting losers get to second base in the parking lot?" Gwen Sanduski peered through the driver's side window. "No offense," she sent to Sam, giving him a sweeter-than-sugar smile.

"I wouldn't dream about edging in on your turf. Is it still five bucks for a BJ or did you have to lower your prices again? I hear Amber Dobson is doing buy-one-get-one free. It's a tough market out there."

Behind Gwen, Amber popped her gum. "Fuck you, Ash."

"Love you, too, bitch."

Gwen rolled her eyes. "Speaking of blowjobs, I heard you finally took Randy into the old locker room."

"Even if I wanted to, I hear you have the place booked through sixth period these days."

"That's not what Randy's saying." Gwen sneered, then she jumped out of the way when Ash whipped the car door open. Gwen stumbled into Amber, and the two clutched at each other to regain their balance.

"Trust me," Ash said, treating herself to one last peek in the rearview mirror, "if I took Randy into the old locker room, you'd know it. He wouldn't be able to walk once I was done with him. *I* don't half-ass anything. I heard Justin Gutierrez said you going down on him was like slathering peanut butter on his balls and letting the dogs go to town. Not sure if I should be more concerned about Justin's proclivities or your technique."

Gwen's eyes tighten into a scowl. "Fuck you, Ash." She jerked her head to Amber, and they stalked off.

Sam watched them disappear around a corner. "Jesus, Ash."

"What?"

"I thought you were friends with Gwen and Amber."

"We are. We're going to the mall together in Arkham next week." She climbed out of the car and slung her bag over her shoulder.

Sam flopped his head onto the headrest and blew out his cheeks. "I don't understand girls."

"You're not supposed to. Oh, are you still coming with me after school?"

"You mean, am I letting you drive my car around town going thrift shopping?"

"That's literally what I just said." Ash beamed at him. "Meet me at the usual."

3

Ash pulled her gym shirt over her head and winced at the stench. She had two sets of gym clothes so she could always have a fresh pair, but she'd forgotten to grab the clean pair on her way out that morning. It was fortunate elective gym class was in the free-weight room, and that place always smelled like sour assholes. She'd probably be safe one more day in the same shirt.

A sardonic tone caught her attention. "Cute top. I just *love* frills." Gwen ran her fingers along the blouse that Sam's mom gave her. "I think I've seen my mom in this same shirt. 'Course, that was in a picture of when *she* was in high school in like the '90s."

Laughter followed Gwen's words, and anger coursed through Ash, and, if she was honest, a little shame. Because Gwen was right. The top was cute, but it was a little dated. The garment either came from the thrift shop or from Alice's own closet. Both sources were known for their outdated fashion, and Ash was familiar with the selections from both. Before she left over ten years ago, Ash's mom used to take her thrift shopping every week. After her mom left, Ash continued to go, but it was Ms. Dyer who took her. Ms. Dyer, herself recently divorced, wanted to keep the tradition alive for the young girl.

Ash snatched the shirt away from Gwen and tossed it in her locker. As always, Gwen was dressed in the latest fashion. Even her workout gear was name-brand.

Ash wasn't poor. Her dad wasn't the city attorney like Gwen's, but he made a great living as one of the few plumbers in town. If Ash wanted to, she could wear the same brands, and Gwen knew it. One reason she didn't was that Ms. Dyer loved buying her clothes. Moms like to go shopping with their daughters, and Alice knew Ash wasn't able to do that anymore. Alice had Sam to shop with, but it wasn't the same buying clothes for a boy, especially one like Sam who was happy to buy the same flannel in three different colors. If Ash only wore name brands, then either Ms. Dyer would feel bad about not being able to afford them or, worse yet, she'd spend more money than she should trying to give Ash that mother-daughter experience she was missing out on.

The other reason Ash didn't dress like Gwen was that it was basic as fuck and Ash had class.

Her gaze took in the entourage of girls arrayed behind Gwen. Most days she counted them as friends, Gwen included. But this was high school, and high school girls were shitty to each other. Ash was self-aware enough to lump herself in with that shitty group, so she didn't think *too* poorly of her friends.

To the degree that their parents' income and/or doting allowed, the other girls' fashion matched Gwen's. Name brands, perfect hair, stylish makeup. Dressed more for a posh photo shoot than for exercise. In fact, in five minutes when the bell rang, the gym would basically transform into a photo studio.

THE ACCURSED

Gym wasn't a mandatory class for seniors, so elective gym attracted a certain type of senior. Rich kids, popular kids, athletes—but not all athletes, just the stars and the hot ones.

Ash closed her locker and turned to face the posse. "Oh, I'm sorry. I didn't get the memo that today was Dress Like Basic Bitch Barbie."

Gasps and laughter met her words in equal measure. Gwen and Amber—for all intents Gwen's shadow—pursed their lips like they'd smelled something rank. Apparently, today wasn't just the standard locker room banter. They were pissed. Ash let it go and headed to the gym, hoping Gwen would let it go, too.

The free-weight room was in a smaller building next to the gymnasium. It had a low roof and no walkway, paved or otherwise, so during the rainy season, the trek to first period was treacherous. The door was usually propped open, allowing the morning air to both defrost the perpetually cold building and drive out the worst of the stench. Ash and the group of girls were the last to arrive.

Even if they arrived after the bell it wouldn't matter much to Ms. Pattinson. In terms of style, appearance, and personality, the elderly gym teacher had more in common with a catcher's mitt than a human. She should have retired before Ash's dad got to high school, but she was perpetual like the black mold that infested the library every winter. She was so old, rumor had it she was in the inaugural class when the school opened in 1874.

Apparently, Mrs. Pattinson used to teach a proper subject, but Ash only knew her as the gym teacher and softball coach. She'd taught Ash's class sex ed when they were freshmen, but when the ancient spinster told the class premarital sex would pave their way to damnation and torment, the district replaced her with someone more...current. Now the aging teacher's presence cursed the Phys Ed department. In the morning, you'd find her in the gym's corner, perched under a yellow flood light like an old iguana.

Mirrors lined the walls, and strength training equipment filled most of the space. Bench presses, leg presses...other types of presses. Ash had no clue what most of them did. Cardio equipment lined the other side of the gym, added a few years ago to encourage more female students to enroll in the class. Ellipticals, stair masters, and treadmills galore. Sexist, perhaps, but it worked. That was where the girls spent most of their time. To be fair, some girls also used the heavier equipment. The beefier cheerleaders who formed the base of the pyramids, for example. Ash used the leg press occasionally, but mostly, she and the others stuck to the cardio machines.

After all, it was easier to talk and check out the guys from that vantage point. Aside from working off her daily McMuffin, that was the primary reason she enrolled in the class.

Ash climbed onto an elliptical, fingers punching in her preferred settings without conscious thought. All hopes of Gwen letting bygones be bygones evaporated a moment later.

"I mean, where did you even find that top? Please tell me your mom bought it for you because I seriously thought you had better taste than that."

Ash's blood pressure rose, and it wasn't because of the warmup cycle on the elliptical.

"Oh, that's right," Gwen continued, though her tone did little to convince anyone that whatever epiphany she had was genuine, "your mom ran off with the mailman." This garnered fewer laughs than Gwen was hoping for but still enough for her to continue.

THE ACCURSED

Ash pumped her legs and cranked on the handles of the elliptical, trying to drown out the sound of Gwen's voice.

"I wonder why anyone would do that, run off with the mailman. Do you think he had a *big package*?"

Ash ground the elliptical to a stop. "What's your problem, Gwen? Listen, I'm sorry if what I said earlier upset you, but bringing my mom into it is really fucked up."

Amber sniggered, but Ash ignored her. Something in Gwen's eyes shifted, and her smile faltered. "Woah, Ash—I didn't mean..." she said, but she mumbled it so no one else could hear. It was the closest to an apology she was going to get.

"Just forget it, okay?" Ash started the elliptical again, but her heart wasn't in it anymore.

The expression Amber shot her made it clear she wasn't ready to give it up, but Gwen jerked her head, and for the next few minutes, it was quiet on the girl's side of the weight room. Flashes from cell phone cameras started strobing, brightening the room like paparazzi had descended on Elsbury High. Now that the Instagramati had worked up a slight glaze—enough to give their skin a beautiful glow, but not enough to make them sweaty and gross—students took a break for their morning selfies.

#CleanLiving
#NaturalGlow
#PainIsWeaknessLeavingTheBody

Hashtag, BasicBitchLife, Ash thought shaking her head as her fellow seniors put themselves in more and more unnatural poses to get the best shot.

The digital masturbation wasn't exclusive to the girls. Just as many of the guys had cell phones in hand. Of course, most of them claimed they were using the pics to check their form...even though every vertical square inch of the gym was reflective for just that purpose.

"Speaking of big packages," Gwen said in a whisper designed for all the girls to hear.

Ash took a deep breath and prepared herself to get suspended that day. It had been a year since she'd been in a fight at school. She promised her dad and Ms. Dyer she wouldn't do it again, but there was only so much shit she was willing to take.

"Have you guys *seen* Konstantin?"

Ash let out her breath, grateful today wasn't the day she broke Gwen's nose. She'd *just* done her nails, so it would have really sucked.

Gwen motioned for the girls to gather around. Ash rolled her eyes. Normally, she was game for gossip, but not so much that day. But she didn't want to start up with Gwen again, so she powered off the elliptical and circled around the gossip queen with the others.

Mrs. Pattinson chose that moment to rouse herself from hibernation. "You should be sweating, ladies."

"Just taking a hydration break, Mrs. Pattinson," Gwen called, but the teacher had already returned to stasis, eyes closed. Gwen lowered her voice. "Have you all seen the new exchange student, Konstantin?"

Dumb question, Ash thought. Elsbury High wasn't so big that you could miss a new student. Besides that, Konstantin, the new exchange student from Russia, was massive. He was one of the tallest guys at the school, and his shoulders were as broad as a tree. She was pretty sure he had to duck to get through doorways. He'd enrolled in Elsbury High in January and wore shorts and T-shirts even when snow blanketed the town.

And he was sooo hairy. Like, teen wolf hairy. His beard was as thick as Principal Mancini's.

"I heard the rugby team calls him the Red Bear," one girl said, and they all giggled.

"I get the bear part, but why red?" Amber asked.

It's a good thing she's pretty, Ash thought.

"Because he's from Russia. Duh," Lisa Herrington answered. Lisa was the smartest girl in school. If Randy Masters's family hadn't donated so much to the district to all but buy him valedictorian, she'd be it. She had to settle for salutatorian, and she was bitter about it. Justifiably so, but at least with the title came a full-ride scholarship to Brown, courtesy of Masters Investment Banking, of course.

"Oh, right." But it was clear Amber had no idea how that answered her question.

Gwen recaptured everyone's attention. "Well, his muscles and beard aren't the only thing about him that's big." Another round of giggles met her words.

"What do you mean?" Lisa asked.

Gwen and Amber shared a glance.

"Let's just say that Amber and I gave Konstantin a warm Elsbury welcome."

"You *didn't*," Ash couldn't help herself.

Elsbury welcome was what they called hooking up in the old locker room. No one remembered the origins of the moniker, but supposedly, it started when the head Elsbury cheerleader hooked up with the

Dunwich quarterback during a homecoming game way back in the day.

Now, it was a term used for anyone hooking up on campus, though most often in the old locker room. Since the new gymnasium was built, the ramshackle old building had been the perfect place for students to slink off. Or toke up, sleep, or basically anything else they wanted to do outside of the watchful gaze of Assistant Principal Sykes.

Gwen nodded, and beside her, Amber followed suit. "It wasn't planned or anything. I was flirting with Konstantin, and one thing led to another. But before I could give him the tour of the old locker room, he invited Amber. Throuples are much more common in Russia, so it wasn't weird or anything."

Ash and Lisa Herrington shared a skeptical glance, but they kept their mouths shut.

"How was it?" someone asked.

"Let's just say that there was plenty of him to go around."

"Oh my god, how did that even work with both of you?"

"Oh my god, how big was it?"

"Oh my god, was it hairy, too?"

The questions came rapid fire.

"Oh my god," Ash said, exasperated by all the giggling, "who cares how big he is?"

The giggles and questions died down.

"Well, of course *you* would say that." Gwen's head and shoulders swayed like she'd just delivered a devastating burn.

"What the hell is that supposed to mean?"

"Obvy, because Randy is packing a Vienna sausage."

THE ACCURSED

Ash's mouth shut with an audible snap, and Gwen looked triumphant. Ash wondered if all of this had been a setup just for that one zinger. Had Gwen and Amber even hooked up with Konstantin?

I wouldn't put it past her, the conniving bitch.

Ash wasn't going to rise to the bait, but before she could return to the elliptical, Amber pointed and laughed. "Just look!"

Ash and everyone else followed the path of her gesture. There were more bench presses than anything over there like biceps and shoulders were the only muscles guys cared about, and every bench was occupied. Once upon a time, the cardio machines faced the walls. But, in a stroke of genius, last year the senior girls flipped them around. They told Mrs. Pattinson facing the mirrors while running was disorienting, but the real reason was they didn't like the idea of the guys ogling them behind their backs.

Also, this way it was easier for the girls to ogle the guys. The gym was a target-rich environment for selfies and hotties. Looking across the gym at the guys, Ash was reminded of this. While the guys certainly took their opportunities for photo ops, they approached the gym much more seriously than the girls. The girls *did* actually exercise…just away from prying eyes. Who wanted to get sweaty and gross where people could see?

Sweaty, bulging muscles met Ash's gaze. The faces the guys made while lifting were hilarious, and the grunting was obnoxious, but she approved of everything else going on over there. The girls' favorite part was when the guys descended on the treadmills. Thin, synthetic athletic shorts, a quick pace, and jouncing cocks.

What wasn't to love?

Right now, the bulk of them were on their backs, heads facing away, so the girls could creep on the fellas without fear of being caught.

And right in the middle of the row of heaving bodies was Randy. Her boyfriend. Randall D. Masters IV.

When her eyes fell on him, a familiar tingle shot through her. They'd been dating since the start of senior year. The longest relationship either of them had ever had. Randy was handsome. Beyond handsome. He was beautiful. Perfect hair, perfect smile, perfect skin. And his body...

Memories of last night flitted through her mind. Randy's hands on her. His hard body pressed against hers. His tongue in her mouth, on her breasts...

Ash shuddered again and hoped no one noticed.

Last night was the closest they had come to having sex. She knew Randy wanted it. He pressed his excitement against her almost every chance he got. Truthfully, she wanted it, too, but she wasn't sure if she was ready for it. They'd done other things. Lots of things. A blush crept up her face at the memories.

Slow and steady wasn't her normal operating speed. She was more of a do-now-and-think-never kind of gal. But taking that final step with Randy was something she couldn't take back, so rather than flying headstrong into a terrible decision—her father's words—she was taking the time to make sure it was what she really wanted.

Still...staring at Randy as he grunted and heaved that bar up and down, his body straining and his abs and pecs taut with effort...it was hard to remember why she kept saying no.

THE ACCURSED

"See what I mean?" The sneer was evident in Gwen's voice. The question knocked Ash out of her reverie. It took an embarrassing amount of time for her to remember what they'd been talking about.

Oh yeah, that's right.

Her boyfriend's tiny penis.

Randy had the face, the hair, and the stature. The body of a Greek god. Unfortunately, like most statues of Greek gods, Randy was...well...

From this vantage it couldn't be clearer how Randy stacked up against the other guys. The thin material of their gym shorts, plus their positions, left little to the imagination. Randy's bulge looked like one of those mushrooms from the Mario games that gave you an extra life.

Beside Randy, as if fate had set him there for a lurid Venn Diagram, was Konstantin. The bulge in the exchange student's shorts was so large it was almost comical.

When Ash turned back, Gwen was smirking.

"See what I mean? The car, the hair, the abs. Gosh, Ash, it's almost like Randy is compensating for something."

Laughter erupted from the girls, loud enough it caught the attention of the guys across the room. Embarrassment twanged through her. Partly for herself, but mostly for Randy. He could be a jerk, but he didn't deserve to be mocked for something he had no control over.

Erika Andres chimed in. "In English class, when we were doing our family trees, Mr. Pinkett made us look up the meaning of our names. Konstantin means 'firm.'" Her smile took to her ears as a blush blossomed on her cheeks.

Gwen and Amber laughed along with the rest of them. Gwen leaned in and whispered so they could all hear it. "Actually, it wasn't that hard. It was big, but soft like a..." Gwen trailed off, at a loss for a comparison.

"An overripe zucchini," Amber supplied triumphantly, then wilted when everyone's eyes turned to her. "What? Haven't you ever held an overripe zucchini? They're super floppy."

A long silence descended on the group.

"Sure," Gwen continued, shaking her head at Amber, "like an overripe zucchini. But still, it hit *allll* the right spots."

Mrs. Pattinson roused and barked at them to get back to work. Ash spent the rest of the period on a machine apart from the others. Her mind whirled back to freshman year sex ed—after Mrs. Pattinson was replaced by someone who'd been sexually active sometime in the past century.

Does size really matter?

The G-spot was only an inch or so deep, so was anything past that really...necessary? Ash wondered, not for the first time, what sex with Randy would be like. Would sex with him be as good as sex with someone like Konstantin? Who knew, maybe Ash was one of those women who couldn't climax from penetration, so it wouldn't matter how Randy measured up.

After all, Randy *was* good with his tongue...

The ringing bell drew her attention back to Randy. She watched him as he racked the barbell and wiped sweat from the bench. He caught her staring at him and smirked. Pointing at himself then her, he pantomimed thrusting his hips, his eyebrows bouncing with each thrust. He jerked his head over his shoulder, toward the old locker room only a stone's throw away.

THE ACCURSED

She blushed at being caught checking him out, but she sent him a reproachful glare. He laughed and joined his friends on their return to the locker room. The smile slipped from her face as she noticed Randy cozying up to a couple girls. She knew Randy was only playing, showing off for his friends, but she wondered how long he'd wait for her to be ready for sex. He was one of the most popular guys in school. She wasn't naïve. She knew he'd had sex before, and she appreciated how patient he had been with her.

But how long will he wait for me?

She wasn't ready, but she didn't want to lose him either.

Am I just being stupid?

They had done so much other stuff together maybe going that last bit wasn't such a big deal.

Ash trudged along the muddy path toward the gym and watched Randy in the distance. As usual, he was the center of attention. Guys and girls, sucked toward him like he had a gravitational pull, hung on his every word.

The knot in her stomach tightened.

4

SAM GOT TO HIS chair just as the bell rang for the start of second period.

"Almost got you, Mr. Dyer," Mr. Pinkett said with a smile. As far as teachers went, Pinkett was pretty cool. He needed new material, though. He loved to call out the students who weren't in their chairs by the bell. Like it'd make the rest of them move faster or something. Not that he ever did anything about it. He was all talk but a cool enough teacher none of the students took advantage of it.

It also didn't hurt that Mr. Pinkett was what Ash called a "silver fox." Most of the girls, and even some of the guys, sat near the front to have an unobstructed view of the study teacher.

"Today we're going to be starting *The Castle of Uldor*, considered one of the first—and best—gothic horror plays."

Loud steps echoed up the steel walkway leading to the portable classroom. A moment later, Randy Masters strode in like he owned the place, his hair still wet from the shower. Sam rolled his eyes. Technically, students didn't get extra time to shower after gym. They had the same seven minutes as students in every other class.

But like most things at Elsbury High—hell, in the whole town of Elsbury—that rule didn't apply to the Masters family.

"Late again, Mr. Masters."

"Sorry, Mr. P, it won't happen again." Randy didn't even glance the teacher's way as he made the same promise he always did. Mr. Pinkett just grunted, stopping his lecture to note Randy's tardiness on the attendance sheet.

Like it'll do any good.

"As I was saying, we're starting *The Castle of Uldor* today—"

Randy slid into his chair next to Sam. "Sick, I love that movie."

Mr. Pinkett's eyes closed like he was making a silent prayer, but he continued despite the interruption. "Unlike the last play, this one we'll be reading aloud in class. I'll assign roles if we don't have volunteers and hold auditions for those thespians among us who vie for the coveted lead roles.

"Before we get to that, I want each of you to open your books and read through the *dramatis personae.* Pay attention to the descriptions, and see if any of the roles really speak to you."

The only response he received was the sound of twenty-four students rolling their eyes in unison. Sam fished the book out of his bag and opened it. He'd already read the play—twice, in fact—but he didn't want Pinkett to think he wasn't following directions. His eyes glanced over the characters and their brief bios. Sam doubted anyone would actually volunteer for a role other than the one or two classmates who were in the drama club.

"Did you go to Fisher's party last weekend?" The sounds of rustling backpacks and the susurration of flipped pages hid the whisper. Veronica Chambers was twisted around in her seat, addressing Randy.

THE ACCURSED

Her hair was wavy and loose, and her breasts practically popped out of her blouse in that position. Sam's heart sped up, and he dropped his head so it wouldn't look like he was checking her out—but not so far that he couldn't see, of course.

"It was wild." Randy's book lay face down on the desk, untouched. "I didn't see you there, though."

"That party was lit." Scott, Randy's ever-present henchman, spun around in the chair in front of Randy.

Veronica rolled her eyes. "I had to visit my grandma in Dunwich. Wish I could have been there."

"Okay, we'll just go in order. Who wants to be the Dowager Countess?" Mr. Pinkett's voice turned Veronica around, but when she noticed he was still at his desk and couldn't see her, she turned back around, dropping her voice.

"What was the occasion?" she asked Randy.

"Mr. Nunez," Pinkett continued. "How about you? I think you'll find the Countess's idiosyncrasies and melodrama to your liking." The students, at least those paying attention, laughed.

"It was his girlfriend's birthday," Scott said, which elicited an *Awwww* out of Veronica. "He was out of town for Valentine's Day, so she said he owed her big time. He went all out. The pool was full of balloons. Wish I saw *you* there," he said, leering at her. Like most people, especially girls, she ignored him.

Veronica was eyeing Randy. "That's really sweet. But it's going to set the bar high for birthdays this year. What are you planning for Ashley? You don't have long to plan, do you?"

Randy leaned back in his chair, the picture of dudebro chill. "Nah, her birthday's not til November. By the time it rolls around next, I'll be across country in college and off the hook."

Veronica's nose scrunched up adorably. "I don't think that's right. Didn't she have a party last year right before summer?"

Randy's face went slack for a moment, then he shook his head. "Nope. Trust me, we've been dating for like five months now. I'd know if it were coming up."

A snort exploded from Sam's nose before he could stop it. All three sets of eyes turned to him. Veronica, noticing him for perhaps the first time in his life, leaned toward him, giving him a magnificent view of her cleavage.

"You're like BFFs with Ash, right? When's her birthday?"

A frown wrinkled Randy's chiseled-from-marble countenance. With a sigh, Sam answered. "Her birthday's in June." And because Randy was a douchelord, Sam continued, "And you've been dating eight months."

Veronica let out a light laugh. "Wow, maybe *you* should be her boyfriend." She smirked at Randy. "Knows her birthday *and* remembers the anniversary."

Scott looked stunned that Sam contradicted Randy.

"It's creepy that you know that, Dyer." Randy looked like he was ready to say more or maybe jump across the aisle and pummel him.

"Something you'd like to share with the class, Mr. Masters?" Mr. Pinkett called. He'd gotten up from his desk and was back at the front of the class again.

THE ACCURSED

Veronica turned her thousand-watt smile on the older man. If Sam were on the other end of one of those smiles, he'd be nothing but a jiggling mass of goo.

Well, maybe one part of me would still be hard.

To his credit, Mr. Pinkett didn't collapse into an amorphous blob, but he looked like his bones went soft. Like he'd been struck by Cupid's arrow...or just got to motorboat a particularly busty stripper.

"Sorry, Doctor Pinkett," she continued, referring to him by his actual honorific. "We were just discussing who should take the role of Professor Drake." Sam's eyebrows rose in surprise, both with how easily she manipulated Pinkett and that she actually did the reading.

Pinkett's face lit up. "Really? Well, that's wonderful! Tell us, which of these strapping lads is going to read the part of the indomitable playboy, William Drake?" His eyes bounced between Randy, Sam, and Scott.

"Playboy?" Randy sat up straight for the first time. "I guess that'd have to be me." He stared at Sam like he was waiting for a challenge, but Sam only shrugged.

Unlike a man-child stuffed into a shirt three sizes too small for him, Sam didn't need to be the center of attention.

"Great!" Pinkett said. "I usually have to assign—"

"Actually, Doctor," Veronica interrupted, "I think Sam should read the role."

For once, Sam and Randy were on the same page. "What?" they said together.

Veronica shot an impish grin at Randy and turned an appraising look on Sam. "Why not? He can play the dashing hero. Underneath that bird's nest and all that flannel he's actually pretty cute."

Sam's insides did something weird. Sam wasn't sure if he had butterflies in his stomach or if he needed to take a crap.

Randy's scowl deepened, if that was even possible. Then he smiled like he was in on the joke. "So what do we do now, audition?"

The butterflies in Sam's stomach melted into cold jelly. Mr. Pinkett clapped his hands, his shoulder-length gray hair waving wildly in his excitement.

"Yes! Randy, why don't you go first. Flip to the opening monologue on page five and read the first paragraph."

Randy grabbed his book and glared at Sam. The meaning was clear: *You're going down.*

Sam made a face, but he wasn't sure if it appropriately conveyed all that he was thinking.

WTF!?

Take it, it's yours!

You're going down, douchebag!

He didn't know where the last thought came from. Reading out loud in front of the whole class was the last thing he wanted to do. The only reason he hadn't spoken up and said so was because Veronica had nominated him.

A stupid smile crept onto his face. *She called me cute.*

Randy cleared his throat with an unnecessarily loud cough. Sam had a lot of practice tuning Randy's voice out, so he didn't hear a word he said. Instead, all he could think about was the smile Veronica gave him when she called him cute. Sam never cared much about his appearance. He wasn't a slob or anything; he combed his hair and wore clean clothes, but outside of that, he spared little attention to fashion trends. Maybe he should start, though. Ash had been begging to give him a makeover for years.

The background noise of Randy's voice trailed off.

Shit, that means it's my turn. What should he do? He didn't want the part, but he couldn't bring himself to forfeit in front of Veronica. Mr. Pinkett considered Randy in silence, his lips pursed. Randy leaned back in his chair, arms behind his head like he'd just delivered the State of the Union to thunderous applause.

"Well, that was...something."

Randy smirked at Sam, preening at his own magnificence.

"But you mispronounced every name except William, and you skipped an entire line of text. Alas, Mr. Masters. You may love the limelight, but sometimes its brightness is too distracting. I think we can safely call it. Congratulations, Mr. Dyer. You'll be our Professor William Drake."

Anger smoldered in Randy's eyes. He wasn't accustomed to losing. Star running back. President of the student body all four years of high school—even as a freshman which was unheard of. He'd been crowned homecoming king every year except sophomore (the year Bobby Winscombe died and they gave it to him posthumously). His father was one of the richest men in town, and Randy wasn't shy about reminding people of that fact.

The Masters family were a bunch of winners. What they wanted, they got. If not by skill, then by guile or commerce.

"Take it from the top, Sam," Mr. Pinkett said. "The first few pages are Drake, so we'll assign the rest of the roles as we come to them."

Great. As if Randy didn't have enough reasons to hate me.

5

Shouts rang out, and car horns blared. The few buses the district owned spewed plumes of exhaust as they sped away from the emptying school.

The sun's heat warmed Ash's back as Randy's tongue scraped against the underside of her own, his hands sliding down to grab her ass.

She had all but forgotten the nastiness with Gwen that morning. After an awkward second period where Gwen and Ash pretended like the other didn't exist, things got mostly back to normal. By lunch, everyone was back to their usual. Ash and Gwen bantered but much friendlier than that morning. Frenemies, if not actual friends.

From behind the pair, Scott snickered.

Ugh, he better not be looking at my ass again.

She lingered in the kiss a moment longer, then shot Scott a withering glance. He had the sense to wipe the sneer off his face and look away. The guy needed to get a life.

Instead of hanging on Randy like some lovesick puppy and checking out my ass when he thinks I'm not looking, he could get his own girl-

friend. She almost shuddered for the poor girl desperate enough to date the skeevy lech.

The sharp tang of cinnamon lingered on her tongue. Randy loved cinnamon-flavored gum, and though she didn't use to like it, she'd acquired the taste.

"You coming over tonight? I got some of that new stuff Scotty was talking about."

Ash had to stop herself from snapping at him. Randy was always trying to get her to come over and try out some new party drug, probably hoping he'd find the right cocktail to finally get her to put out. She'd told him a thousand times she wasn't into that. "Sorry, I'm going shopping today. Remember?"

Before he could answer, Randy stiffened, but not in the good way. "Jesus, what is with this guy?"

Following his gaze, she saw Sam approaching, a frown Randy's equal on his own face. "What's wrong?"

Randy disentangled himself from her embrace. "Nothing. He's just always around. He follows you like some lost puppy. I just wish it could be the two of us for once."

Ash's eyes flicked toward Scott, but she didn't point out the irony. "You know we're just friends. Besides, we barely hang out at school."

"What, like it's better that you spend all your time outside of school with him?"

"You know that's not true. So, come on, what's really going on?" She dropped her voice so Sam wouldn't overhear.

Instead of answering, Randy raised his voice so Sam could hear. "Hey, babe, here comes your lost puppy."

THE ACCURSED

Unsurprisingly, Randy's comment garnered a guffaw out of Scott. "Careful, you don't want him to beat you up."

Randy barked a laugh. The captain of the rugby team, scared of little Sammy Dyer? "Like that would ever happen."

Scott's voice dropped as Sam neared. "Remember what happened in eighth grade? Dude's crazy…"

Randy laughed again, but his eyes narrowed, and he wrapped his arms around Ash tightly.

Is he…jealous? There was no way. Randy was the most popular guy in school, had been since he stepped foot in Elsbury High. He was handsome, rich, and dated the prettiest girls—present company included. Sam was…well, Sam. He was smart, but not top-of-class. Cute, but in a dorky kind of way. He could be one of those nerds in a teen rom-com who got a makeover and the heroine realized he's always been the perfect guy for her.

She had to fight the urge to snort at the thought. If Sam had more confidence, maybe did something with that mop of brown hair, and at least put in a *little* effort, he'd probably have a girlfriend. *For a guy with a girl as a best friend you'd think he'd have all the know-how to maximize his assets.* But the kid was hopelessly—*frustratingly*—inflexible.

She came to a decision. When they were out shopping today, she'd pick out some new clothes for him—clothes that would accentuate his assets rather than cover them up with layers of denim and thick, patterned cotton, and she wouldn't rest until he agreed to try them on.

No one would know it by looking at him, but he actually has a killer bod. She was reminded of it every time he came over to swim. He had always been a scrawny kid, but he packed on some muscles sophomore year. At the time, she hoped Sam would grow more confident, but if anything, he spent even more effort blending in. If he weren't so damned shy, she wouldn't be the only person at school who knew it.

Sam smiled, but he looked like he caught a whiff of something rotten. "Ready to go?"

"Where are you two going?" A hint of accusation tinged Randy's question. "I thought we were hanging out after school."

"I told you I was going shopping today. Remember?"

"You didn't say you'd be going with *him*."

Ash crossed her arms. "Do you want to come instead?" Surprise, and a little hurt, flitted across Sam's face.

"I don't wanna go shopping. *I've* still got a pair." Randy sneered and grabbed his crotch.

She slapped his arm. "You're such a jerk sometimes. I'll call you later, okay?"

Randy nodded, and after giving her one last long kiss, he and Scott took off.

"Well, that was charming," Sam said once the two were gone.

"Give it a rest." It was bad enough that she had to deal with one moody guy in her life.

"You sure you wouldn't rather go shopping with Randy? When you're done, he could take you to the mall. I hear that's where all the cool kids hang out."

Ash winced, realizing she probably shouldn't have offered to ditch Sam to go shopping with Randy. She linked arms with him. "There was no chance in hell he was going to agree to go thrifting with me."

THE ACCURSED

Sam pulled his arm free from her grasp and headed toward the parking lot. "Let's just go." He didn't offer to let her drive this time and set about coaxing the old beater to life.

A sullen silence descended on the car while they waited for the long line of vehicles to file out of the school parking lot. It dragged on for minutes until she couldn't take it anymore.

"My god, you're such a little bitch sometimes. Just *say* it already."

He wasn't going to make it that easy though, the prima donna. "Say what?"

"Whatever's chapping your ass."

Outside the window, the middle and elementary schools slid by. Traffic finally thinned a few blocks later. Sam navigated toward the strip mall near the highway to Dunwich.

"I've got nothing to say."

Ash let it drop. If he wanted to play the silent game, she could play it, too. Minutes passed, the silence only broken by their breathing. Well, and also the cacophony of sounds emanating from the car. The thing was a mobile orchestra of dings, cracks, and pops.

"He's a fucking Neanderthal."

Her heart skipped a beat at the sudden outburst.

"Who?"

"Randy. He's such a douche. All he cares about is looking cool, and he treats you like a trophy."

"First off, have you seen me? I *am* a fucking trophy." He chuckled, and some of the tension leaked out of the atmosphere. "Second, he doesn't like doing stuff like this."

"Like what?"

"Shopping. Thrifting. You know."

"Stuff that you like to do, you mean?"

"He's a guy."

"*I'm* a guy."

Ash threw her hands in the air. "But he's my *boyfriend*. You're just my friend."

"There's a difference?"

"You'd know there is if you sacked up and asked Veronica out."

That shut him up real quick. The right side of his face flushed, and he stared out the window for a few moments before responding, "We're not talking about me right now."

"I'm just saying... It's different. *We're* friends. Randy's my boyfriend. It's a different dynamic. By the way," she said, hoping to change the topic away from her boyfriend's many faults, "I heard Veronica talking about you today in the bathroom."

For a moment, she didn't think he was going to take the bait.

"You did? What'd she say?"

"I knew it!" She pumped her fist in the air. "You're still totally in love with her!"

"I *am not*," he said with little conviction.

"You totally are!"

"Are you going to tell me what she said or not?"

"Depends. Are you going to admit that you've got the hots for her?" Sam let out a long breath but stayed quiet. "Then nope, I'm not gonna say anything."

She sat back in the rickety chair and crossed her arms. She would eventually tell him what Veronica said, but she'd let him stew in misery for a while. Maybe it would teach him not to mouth off.

THE ACCURSED

The car ride lapsed into silence again until they pulled into the strip mall. A long, low building stretched into an "L", home to a thrift store, a greasy spoon diner, what passed for an arts and crafts store—but was really just a place for the local spinsters to quilt and gossip—and a storefront that had been empty as long as Ash could remember.

It was habit to help the seatbelt spindle back into the frame. Otherwise, it would have dangled out of the car, and Sam would insist on putting it back in place before they did anything else.

"You know," Sam said before she climbed out, "I may not know much about relationships, but you'd think with Randy leaving town for Spring Break that he'd want to spend as much time with you as possible."

Ash opened her mouth to tell him to mind his own business, but the words wouldn't come. The Tercel's door rebounded back toward her when she shoved harder than necessary and got out.

6

The bell above the door to Heavenly Treasures chimed as Ash entered. The door bumped against a stack of boxes and came to a sudden stop.

"Woah," Ash said, stopping with one foot over the threshold. More boxes blocked her view of the interior. Heavenly Treasures was no stranger to clutter, but she'd never seen it like this.

Sam came up behind her and peered over her shoulder. "What happened here?"

A muffled voice called from somewhere near where the cash register should be. "Sorry, don't mind the mess!"

Judy, the owner, popped up from behind the counter, running the back of a hand over her brow. Her hair was in disarray, and glasses sat askew on the bridge of her nose. A wide smile blossomed on her face when she caught sight of the two of them.

"Oh, Ashley, dear. How lovely to see you." Her gaze shifted to Sam, and her grin grew wider. "Goodness! Samael, dear boy! You're getting bigger and more handsome every time I see you."

Sam stepped around Ash and made his way through the maze of boxes to give her a hug. "Hi, Judy."

The older woman pulled him into a hug. "A lot can change in a few months, Sammy. Especially for you young folk." She released him, and her hands squeezed his biceps, then she turned to Ash with a secretive grin on her face.

Ash rolled her eyes. "What's all this?" She let the door close behind her, and she made her way through the mess. None of the boxes were labeled, but they were all brand-new. The thrift store got its share of large donations, usually when someone old passed away, but those boxes were usually old and musty, and sometimes, so were the contents.

The bell above the entrance tinkled, and the door swung open until it met the same box Ash had hit. An elderly woman's face peered around the door.

"Sorry, Dottie," Judy called. "Watch your step as you come round." She finally released Sam from her appraising gaze and returned to the safety behind the counter, taking a long draft from a coffee mug before she answered Ash. "We got an estate donation."

"Oh no," she said, though she wasn't surprised given the number of boxes. "I hadn't heard of anyone passing recently."

"You probably wouldn't have heard about this one. They lived in Dunwich."

"That's too bad." Sam lifted one of the cardboard lids and peered inside at the assorted bric-a-brac.

Dottie stopped her own review of a box's contents and pulled her hands away. "Dunwich? Isn't that where that couple died?"

"Oh, Dottie, mind your gossip! I got a fresh batch of Harlequins the other day, so go at 'em." She waved, shooing the older woman away. Dottie harrumphed and tottled toward the back of the store.

THE ACCURSED

Sam returned the lid to the box. "What happened in Dunwich?"

"Tragic." Judy shook her head but didn't elaborate further. "What are you looking for today, dearie?" She didn't bother asking Sam. Ash had been shopping at Heavenly Treasures since she was a kid. Hell, even before that. When she was in utero. Her mom and Sam's mom had been shopping here since they were young.

"Just browsing today. I wasn't able to make it in last week, so I wanted to see what was new. Oh, and to get something for Alice." Her fingers found the hem of the blouse Alice had given her. Ash's mom and Alice used to go thrift shopping with their moms. It was a ritual both women carried over when they had their own children.

Sam had lost his interest in shopping a long time ago, but Ash still loved it despite the painful memories it dredged up. After her mom left, Ash probably would have given up on the tradition as well, but Alice stepped in to keep the tradition alive. It helped both of them grieve and move past losing people they loved.

Judy smiled. "Oh, Lord knows there are always more treasures coming in. You know where everything is, so just shout out if you need help."

Sam and Ash separated, each of them going their own way. Just like her, Sam had spent many of his formative years in Heavenly Treasures. The style of the clothes and the sophistication of the electronics may have changed, but it was still the same store. He knew where to find his favorite stuff. Sam loved perusing the old books and motley assortment of weird knickknacks. They were fascinating to browse, no doubt, but Ash knew why he really liked them. It was the ladders.

The perimeter of Heavenly Treasures was lined with floor-to-ceiling shelves, which were full to bursting with *stuff*. The only reliable way to get a good look at it all was to use the rolling library ladders.

Sam raced off toward the nearest ladder, and Ash and Judy shared a look of exasperated amusement.

Ash probably knew the shop better than anyone except Judy. She tried to come in every week to see what was new and to visit with the woman who was almost like a grandma to her. Spending so much time in Heavenly Treasures over the years, Ash had seen innumerable family heirlooms and prized possessions get donated because surviving family members thought it was junk. She didn't want her stuff to end up like that, so she rarely bought anything for herself.

When Amanda Williams had run off, Ash had inherited the "craft room." No crafting ever happened in it. It was simply a room full of all the junk she collected over the years. Luckily, Ash didn't inherit her mother's knack for hoarding junk.

Today she was looking for clothes. She was telling the truth when she said she wanted to get something for Ms. Dyer, but ever since she'd had the thought earlier, she couldn't shake the urge to buy a few new outfits for Sam.

It's a good thing he's over there pretending to be Belle from Beauty and the Beast. That'll keep him out of my hair while I shop. There's no way he'd let her if he knew. The stubborn boy saw nothing wrong with the way he dressed. And, in truth, there was nothing *wrong* with his wardrobe. It could just be...better.

Unfortunately for Sam, Ash wouldn't be able to stop thinking about giving him a makeover, so her secret mission to shop for him was going full steam ahead. Convincing him to try them on would be a problem for later.

Thirty minutes later, Ash dropped a pile of clothes on the counter, and a small pile of paper tags followed suit. It was faster to collect them while she shopped rather than have Judy root through the pile at the register. It was a simple system. All the clothes had different colored tags, and each color represented a different price. Judy nodded her thanks and collected the tags.

"What's all that?"

Shock and guilt blazed through her in equal measures when Sam spoke from behind her. Most of the clothes were obviously men's, and a frown crinkled his eyebrows when he spotted them.

"J-Just some things for my dad and Alice." While Sam had broad shoulders, her dad was significantly larger than him. With a shrug, Sam turned to peruse a shelf of glass baubles nearby.

The shushing sound of paper hitting the floor caught her attention, and Ash noticed a tag at her feet. Bending down to grab it, her butt hit a stack of boxes. It teetered, then toppled before she could steady it.

"Jeesh, Ash. Lay off the Toaster Strudels."

She whirled on him. If her finger were a knife, she'd have skewered him with it. "Watch it, buddy, or you'll be drinking your strudels through a straw when your jaw is wired shut." Sam raised his hands in mock surrender and bent over to help clean up. Ash twisted and gave her ass a cursory glance before helping him.

Still got it.

Luckily, most of the box was clothing. She picked up a burnt orange vest that crunched under her fingers like velvet. Underneath was a matching one in maroon. Images of her dad in grade school flitted through her mind, and a shiver ran up her spine.

"Too bad those things went out of style," Sam said, righting the box and getting ready to dump an armload of other vests back into it.

"Wait." A flash of color toward the bottom of the box caught her eye. The clothes had shifted when the box fell, exposing the corner of an ornate wooden frame. She pulled it out, careful in case it was fragile. She needn't have worried, though. Inside the heavy frame was a painting on thick canvas.

Sam dumped the last few clothes back in the box. "What's that?"

She shrugged and turned it so he could see it. It was old. She didn't know anything about art, but she could see the fine cracks in what she guessed was acrylic paint. In it, two people lay in the grass, bodies intertwined in an embrace. Leaves and branches covered their naked bodies, and a large, gnarled tree stood sentinel above them, its branches reaching into the dark sky. It was nighttime in the painting, the colors muted. The tree's leaves were different shades of dark greens, oranges, and reds. A piece of blue painter's tape was stuck on the bottom of the canvas with the words DONATE written in black marker.

Sam made an appreciative noise. "Kinky."

Ash slapped him on the arm. "Perv."

"You're the one looking at an ancient Playboy."

"It's art. It doesn't count as porn."

"Let me see." Looming above them from the other side of the counter, Judy held her hand out. "Ashley's right, Sam. It's art, so it doesn't count as pornography." Ash made a face at him. "But he's right, too," Judy said, taking off her glasses. "Doing the hanky-panky in the woods like that is pretty kinky."

THE ACCURSED

Sam gave her a dose of her medicine, making the same face.

"I remember when my Jonathan was still alive, we used to—"

"Judy!" Ash's cheeks burned. Judy may not have been family, but she was close enough—and old enough—that Ash didn't want to hear the sordid details.

"What?" She noticed Sam covering his ears and Ash's blush. "Oh, grow up you two. You're both adults now."

Sam struggled to speak through his giggles. "Yeah, but you could be our grandma."

"And what's that supposed to mean? Geezers can't have needs, Sam Dyer?"

Dottie shuffled into the aisle. "I could tell you stories of the old folks' home..."

Sam's chuckles turned into outright laughter. "Please don't," he begged.

The older women shared a glance, shaking their heads in exasperation. Judy turned the painting over to reveal that it had a solid wood back. She turned it over again and ran her fingers along a small mark in the corner. Her brow furrowed. "I think I recognize this. I think I do, at least. It's been a while since I've seen one."

"It's not an original?" Ash's heart sank. If it were a print or a duplicate, it wasn't as special.

"I think it is. My mother had something similar. The people were...similarly occupied as these."

"There's got to be tons of smutty paintings out there."

Judy nodded. "And no doubt you're right, Sammy boy. But *this*..." She ran a fingertip over the mark and showed it to them. Two circles, one inside the other with a small dot in the center. "My mother's had this same symbol. She got it from my mormor when she married my father."

Ash asked before Sam could, "What's a mormor?"

"Sorry, got caught up in memories there. It means 'grandma.' My mother was born in Sweden." She turned back to the painting, and her eyes went distant. "I forget exactly what she called it, but it would bring the newlyweds good luck and a bountiful harvest."

"Your parents were farmers?"

Everyone fell silent, then Sam leaned close to Ash and stage whispered, "She means it was supposed to make them have lots of babies." He jerked out of her reach before she could hit him.

"It was just old wives' tales. You know, like hanging sprigs of rosemary in the rafters to keep evil spirits away. My mormor emigrated from Trosa many years ago. She was very superstitious. Always going on about goblins and demons. Her English wasn't very good. Do you want it, dear?"

Ignoring Sam's chuckling, Ash took the painting back from Judy. "Sure." Sam wouldn't let her hear the end of it anytime soon, but she didn't rise to the bait.

Whatever, it wasn't like she even wanted kids. *It's just a pretty, romantic painting.*

7

They got back to Ash's just after sunset. Heavenly Treasures was the only thrift store in town, but there was another in Dunwich that Ash just *had* to hit up. Sam had a general rule about not taking longer trips in his beat-up Tercel, but Ash begged until he relented—with the caveat that she wasn't allowed to drive.

Mr. Williams' eyes widened when he caught sight of the day's haul. "What's all this?"

Ash scurried up the stairs without glancing at her dad, so Sam answered, "You're getting a new wardrobe."

Mr. Williams' eyes narrowed at his daughter's back. She must have felt the glare because she called over her shoulder, "Show you later. We'll be in my room."

With an apologetic shrug, Sam trudged upstairs with his own armload of bags. The bags plopped to the floor; Sam followed suit and fell into a large pink beanbag chair. "Your dad doesn't seem too excited to get new clothes."

Ash set her own bags on the chair in the corner and turned to him with a sheepish expression. "About that..."

Sam narrowed his eyes at the sheepish look of innocence Ash was trying on. "Don't tell me..."

"I knew if I said anything you wouldn't let me!"

"Well, duh! That should've been your first hint. My clothes are *fine*. Why do people keep giving me such a hard time about this lately?"

"Who else is saying you dress like an emo lumberjack?"

"Ha ha. Just forget it."

Ash scanned through the bags, pulling out bundles of folded clothes and organizing them into piles. "If you must know, I got the idea from something Veronica said today."

That caught his attention. Sam perked up.

"She mentioned you'd be cuter if you paid a little more attention to your wardrobe."

"Those were her exact words?" He tried to keep his tone from sounding too excited.

Ash's gaze fell onto the ceiling while she recalled the other girl's words. "She said, 'I'd totally let Sam rail me if he wore anything other than flannel 24/7.'"

"Shut up!" He picked up one of Ash's dozens of throw pillows and threw it at her. "Did she actually say something or not?"

She held up her hands in surrender and to protect from additional projectiles. "Okay, okay! Don't get your panties in a bunch. She said something like, 'Underneath all that flannel, Sam is actually kinda cute.'"

"She said that? Those exact words?"

The grin on Ash's face grew to an almost maniacal size.

THE ACCURSED

"Oh, shut up!" He tried, but he couldn't quite wipe the stupid smile from his face. Crossing his arms, he pretended to be interested in the far side of the room. "Like I care about what she thinks."

"Liar."

She probably made it up just to justify buying me new clothes...or maybe so I'd finally have the balls to ask Veronica out. He wouldn't put it past her to make something up like that. She'd been nagging him to let her give him a makeover for years, at least since the summer before freshman year.

'New school, new look, new you', was what she said. But 14-year-old Sam was too shy for such drastic changes. Puberty had been a real bitch, and the soon-to-be-freshman was clinging to anything that was the same.

That was a long time ago, though. He wasn't that scared little boy anymore.

Then again...he hadn't changed much since then, so was he still that same little kid?

Maybe it wouldn't hurt to at least see what she had in mind...

"Yes!" Ash pumped her fist. "I knew you'd come around."

"I didn't say yes."

"I know that look."

"The look of 'it would just be faster to give Ash what she wants than to argue with her all night.' That look?"

She snapped her fingers and pointed at him. "That's the one."

The bags disgorged more and more clothes. While Ash busied herself with organizing the contents—it did actually look like she bought clothes for her dad and Alice, so she wasn't a complete liar—Sam riffled through the bag nearest him. Aside from a small glass animal he thought his mom would like, the only other item in it was the painting Ash bought. He chuckled at the idea of her buying some ancient fertility charm. If this were some cheesy romance book, he'd think Ash was trying to nail down the town's most eligible rich guy by getting pregnant.

Looking at the painting, he had to give her at least some credit. The painting *was* beautiful. *Maybe a little haunting, too.* He'd seen enough art where the people looked like shapeless lumps of dough or like kindergarteners had drawn them to appreciate when an artist could do it right.

He wondered how old it was. Judy said her grandma had something similar, and Judy was pretty up there, so that could have put Judy's somewhere in the 1800s. He was no expert, but it didn't look like it was the worse for it. The layered paint was cool and oily under his fingertips. His thumb brushed the strip of tape with DONATE written on it. Carefully, without scratching the painting, he worked at the corner until it came up. Girding himself to earn Ash's wrath if he destroyed her new painting, he pulled the tape free a millimeter at a time, eyeing it to ensure none of the paint came free. The fresh tape pulled away with ease and curled into a corkscrew when it came free.

The persnickety tape clung to his hand, and when he tried to peel it off, it only transferred to the other. "Get off me, you little shit."

"What was that?"

"Nothing," he mumbled, ridding himself of the tape at last by brushing his hand on the bed and leaving the sticky ball attached to Ash's comforter.

Finally rid of the nuisance, he turned back to the painting. "Hey, check this out."

THE ACCURSED

A true lover's kiss to bestow Her blessing

The words were written in a thick, curling script, followed by three initials.

Ash's fingers brushed the newly revealed text. "P.H.L."

"You better get Randall over here so you can bestow a *blessing* on him."

"Shut *up!*" She swiped at Sam like he was a bothersome insect, whatever reverence that had come over her while reading the inscription disappearing like it'd never been there.

Rolling out of the beanbag chair, Sam jumped to his feet and circled to the other side of the bed. "What? You don't want to be fruitful with him? I figure with this thing you could pop out a little Randall Masters the fifth by next year."

"You are such an ass." She stalked around the bed toward him, but he paced her, keeping the bed between them. "It's already April, dumb ass. I couldn't give birth by December. Didn't you pay attention in sex ed?"

"I remember condoms and consent, but I must have been absent when they covered true love and mystical blessings." He held the painting out and yanked it away when she reached for it. "Where's your true lover now?"

With something bordering between a laugh and a battle cry, she leapt onto the bed, her momentum carrying her to the other side before Sam could get the headboard between them. She caught him around the waist and threw him down onto the beanbag. Sam cowered behind the painting like it was a shield.

"You know," she said, trying to find an opening in his defenses to pinch or poke him, "I remember a certain little boy professing his undying love for me." Spotting an opening, she jabbed her finger into his ribs, laughter exploded unbidden from Sam's mouth. "He was *so* polite."

Jab.

"So romantic."

Jab.

"Told me I was his one true love."

Jab.

"And said he'd marry me one day."

Tickling had always been his Kryptonite. After a few long moments of torture, she finally eased the assault. Tears of mirth streamed down his face, and the laughter trickled to a stop like water chugging out of a bottle. Finally able to think—and breathe!—again, memories flitted through his mind.

When the Williams had a girl and the Dyers a boy, it was only a matter of time before they started joking about little Samael and Ashley getting married one day. They had grown up with the constant jokes, and at some point, the two little kids started to believe it. When they played house, they were husband and wife. And instead of playing cops and robbers, they played Bonnie and Clyde.

The naivete of youth, he thought and said as much.

Ash narrowed her eyes. "What's that supposed to mean?"

"Nothing," he said quickly. "Just that if I'd known then how time and gravity would ravage you, then I wouldn't have been so quick to propose marriage."

"That's it!" She yanked the painting out of his hands and tossed it on a pile of clothes. Without the protection of her beloved painting,

Sam was at her mercy. She pinned him with her knees, poking, pinching, and tickling until he begged her to stop.

"No, not my underarms!"

"Say I haven't been ravaged by gravity or time!" She dug her fingertips into his ribs.

Air wheezed out of his lungs, and his face hurt from smiling. Finally, she relented enough so he could catch his breath.

"Okay," he gasped, taking in a lungful of air. "Okay, okay. I surrender."

"*Say it.*" She curled her fingers into claws.

The words spilled from Sam's mouth in a rush. "It's a good thing you got the love spell. Otherwise, your true love would take one look and—" He didn't have time to finish. Ash dug her fingers into his ribs, his sides, and underarms.

Sam didn't have the energy to fight back. Knees pinned his hands down, and she pressed on his shoulders with her hand so he couldn't wriggle out of her grasp.

When he finally blinked the tears from his eyes, he saw an unreadable expression on her face. "What's up?"

The pressure on his shoulders eased a bit, and Ash sat up. Sam didn't dare let himself relax, though. He'd fallen for her tricks too many times before. In the blink of an eye, he could again be at her mercy.

"Can you imagine if Randy *was* my true love? How sad would that be?"

Sam didn't know what to say to that, and Ash looked like she was lost in thought, so he took some time to formulate a response. "You guys have been dating forever." It had only been eight months, but in high school time, it may as well have been forever.

Her mouth opened, but whatever she was going to say didn't come out. The pensive expression slipped from her face, replaced by one much more familiar—mischief. Ash squared her shoulders and threw out her hands, announcing in a grand, imperious tone, "I'm afraid the fates have decreed the only man worthy of my hand is Sir Samael Dyer the Brave."

A laugh burst from him, straight from his stomach.

Man, I haven't thought about Sir Samael Dyer the Brave and Lady Ashley Williams the Fierce since we were...eight?

The two wayward adventurers had traveled the land, ridding the kingdom of evil, and—

His reminiscing thoughts were hijacked when Ash leaned down and planted a kiss on his lips.

8

Before Sam registered what had happened, Ash hopped off the beanbag and danced away, laughing and twirling like she was an eight-year-old girl again. Just like when they were kids, when they knew kissing was something grownups did but they hadn't grasped the meaning behind it. One of them would run up to the other, plant a kiss on their cheek, and run away giggling, the other in hot pursuit. They hadn't played that game since the second or third grade, so Ash planting a kiss on Sam now was...unexpected.

Not just unexpected. Earth-shattering.

He and Ash had always been close. They shared a blanket when watching movies... walked arm-in-arm. Their closeness raised more than a few eyebrows, and rumors about their relationship had plagued them for years, but they'd never been anything other than friends. Best friends.

Sam had given up on hoping for more a long time ago.

Mr. Williams' comments that morning floated back to him. He had scolded Ash for wearing so little in front of Sam because, in Mr. Williams' mind, Sam was a potential suitor. Then for him to turn around and tell Sam to hold in there, that Ash would come around.

It had been…uncomfortable to be reminded of the feelings he had for Ash.

No, he thought. *The feelings I* used *to have for her.*

Seeing Ash in her undies was nothing new to him. Hell, her swimsuits were more provocative, but years of bottling up any attraction he had for her had conditioned him not to notice. He was no longer plagued by pangs of jealousy seeing her on another guy's arm or listening to yet another recounting of her hooking up with her latest boyfriend.

He had grown blind to the feelings. Much in the same way he no longer noticed all the creaks, squeals, and rattles of the Tercel. It was never going to change, so there was no point in paying attention to it.

And then she kissed him.

Sure, they'd kissed before. Given each other pecks on the cheek occasionally for birthdays or Christmas, that sort of thing. But a kiss on the lips, and with her straddling him like that…

A maelstrom of thoughts and emotions swirled through Sam too quickly for him to make sense of anything.

A motion caught his attention. Ash has stripped off her pants and was slipping a skirt over her legs, one she'd picked up at the thrift store in Dunwich. He caught a brief glimpse of her panties before the skirt was over her hips.

She turned from side to side, inspecting her reflection in the mirror. "What do you think?" She was focused on the mirror, so she didn't see his expression, which he imagined looked something like a frog that had eaten a particularly homicidal wasp.

"Um…" His thoughts were still churning like a life raft stuck in river rapids.

THE ACCURSED

With a scrunch of her nose, she shook her head. "God, why am I asking *you* for fashion advice?" She didn't wait for a response, slipping the skirt off and stepping out of it.

Try as he might, he couldn't avert his eyes. It was a small room and hard to ignore all the commotion. The Styrofoam pellets in the beanbag squealed as he leaned back, trying to put some distance between the two of them. But that only put Ash—and her unintended strip tease—in his direct line of sight. In a burst of inspiration, he grabbed the painting and pretended to study it.

Right, because I've always been such an art aficionado. Smooth, Sam.

The gaudy, ornate frame did a great job blocking her increasing nudity…and his increasing arousal.

Jesus, what is wrong with me?

Ash was his best friend. The sight of her in her underwear shouldn't arouse him. She was pretty, sure, but he didn't think of her as a *girl*. Not anymore. *She's just Ash.* His friend. His partner in crime. His buddy.

"I need the full-length mirror." Her words burst his spiraling thoughts like a dart through a balloon. With an armload of clothes, Ash headed to the bathroom. The second story of the house was much smaller than the bottom. There was just enough space for her bedroom, bathroom, and a vestigial attic that was more broom closet than anything. She called back over her shoulder, "See how those clothes fit."

"Um… Yeah, okay." He had no intention of trying on any clothes. The last thing he wanted was to disrobe while in his current…*state*.

Now that she was gone, he no longer needed the painting to hide his traitorous erection. The painting bounced when he tossed it on the bed. He messed up the neat pile of clothes she'd laid out for him to make it look like he'd done what she asked.

Get it together, Sam. This isn't your first accidental boner. Nothing new, just find a distraction.

His gaze fell on the old school radio, long forgotten on a shelf under a large bay window. With a crackle and pop, the retro device came to life. Most of the stations it was likely to pick up came from Dunwich. Dunwich wasn't that far, not as the bird flew at least, but Elsbury had notoriously poor reception despite the fact that it was separated from Dunwich by only forests, grasslands, and low hills. So it was only on clear days that the thing could pick up Dunwich stations.

It should have been possible to pick up some from Arkham, too, but that was a rare occasion. Like, all nine planets aligned rare. Otherwise, it was just local stations. *Three* local stations, to be exact. Two were legit stations, in that they had hosts and programming and music. News mostly, a smattering of national, but mostly local. Advertisements, talk radio. Once a week they broadcasted open mic night at the local pub.

A third station was operated by some crackpot in the hills above town. The frequency changed daily, and you'd never hear music. Or news. As far as Sam could tell it was 24 hours of the host rambling. Sometimes it sounded like he was speaking in tongues. How the host had time to record it all Sam had no idea, but it was always on for anyone who wanted to listen and persistent enough to find the day's frequency.

When Sam and Ash were freshmen, they had listened to the station for two whole days. They pounded back soda and coffee, determined to stay awake for the host to take a break. But they failed, falling asleep after 49 hours. And when they awoke eight hours later, the host was still talking.

With every turn of the dial, static popped. He had to go through the range of frequencies twice before he finally found it. A shiver ran up his spine as the host's deep, emotionless voice came out of the speakers.

"—will feed her cat ocean fish paté for dinner even though Truffles has told her no fewer than seven times chicken and gravy is his favorite."

Sam laughed and shook his head. It had been years since he'd listened, but it was the same crazy stuff.

"In 147 hours, the harbinger cometh. The four C's are our only hope. Community, charity, carrots, and—"

"Anything good on?"

Sam jumped about three feet in the air. Ash dropped a large stack of clothes by the now-empty shopping bags, and a smaller stack went into the laundry hamper. She was wearing pajamas—a pair of gray Victoria's Secret sweats and matching top. Sam couldn't help noticing how the pajamas hugged her curves and how the shirt left a wide expanse of flat stomach exposed. A tingling sensation ran up his spine.

Her brows crinkled, and she plopped onto the bed, crossing her legs and hugging a pillow to her chest like she was hiding behind it.

Crap—did she notice him looking? *Can this day get any more awkward?*

He turned back to the radio, but before he could comment on the lack of selection, Ash cried out.

"What did you do?" She held the painting out like an accusation. He didn't notice it at first, but then he saw it. The frame had split along the back.

It must have happened when I threw it on the bed.

"Shit, Ash. I'm so sorry. Can we fix it?" She handed it over, and he inspected it. Sam spent a lot of time playing with Legos as a kid, and as he grew, his interest morphed into more complicated hobbies like building computers, model airplanes, and other such things. He was good with his hands. If either of them could fix the frame, it would be him.

The panel that made up the back had popped out, one corner protruding like it no longer fit properly. He hoped he could just pop it back into place, but as soon as he removed his thumbs, it flexed back out.

"Careful!"

"Guess it won't be that easy. Does your dad have any wood glue?"

"I'm not sure."

"We could just leave it. The frame is still structurally sound." Sam applied pressure to the frame, trying to bend it. It didn't move.

"No, it won't lie right against the wall. But what if we took that piece off?"

There weren't any nails or staples. If ancient glue was the only thing holding it together, he could probably pry it off with no issues.

The thin sheet of wood squeaked as he worked his fingertips under it, and with barely a tug, the panel peeled off with a hollow *thump*.

"Shit!" She fumbled to catch it, but the thin panelboard bounced off her hand and spun to the floor.

THE ACCURSED

"Woah, look at this." Sam angled the frame so the light caught it. Words were scrawled across the canvas in black ink in two different handwritings and what looked like two different languages. The writing was old, probably as old as the painting itself. He didn't know how he knew it, but he did. It was probably the flowing, curly handwriting. *People just don't write like that anymore.*

"What language is this in?" he wondered.

"English, duh."

Sam shook his head but didn't rise to the bait. "Not that. *This* one."

"I'm *barely* passing English. You think I can identify a foreign language? Who am I, Dr. Daniel Jackson?"

The script at the top of the canvas had some English letters, but there were some weird ones too. "Greek? Russian, maybe?"

"Again, you're asking the wrong person. But I think you're focusing on the wrong thing. What does the English say?"

The loopy script made his eyes itch. The squiggly loops swam in his vision like he was looking at one of those Magic Eye pictures that were so popular in grade school. Just like one of those trippy pictures, it took Sam a minute of staring before the words fell into recognizable patterns.

True love's kiss to begin anew
Issue, Bounty, and Love be Blessed
Cleave, unite, ere new moon
Else fields and house will lay in Death

"That's a shitty poem. It doesn't even rhyme right. And they spelled 'ear' wrong."

"*Ere* means 'before,'" he explained. "In this case, 'before the new moon.'"

"That doesn't even make sense." Ash sounded a little disappointed. "Why would you cut something and then put it right back together?"

Sam looked at her in surprise.

"What?"

"Nothing," he said. "I'm just surprised you know what cleave means."

"Asshole!"

Sam just nodded, not arguing the point. "This is Early Modern English. Well, not exactly. It's—"

"Sorry, Professor Dyer. I don't really care."

He growled and continued, "Cleave can also mean...like...to stick or adhere. This is a love poem, so I'm going to go out on a limb and say it means to consummate the relationship. To have sex."

"I *know* what consummate means."

"I'm just making sure." But the grin he shot her was anything but innocent.

"Kissing, sex, bounty. So, what is this, an ancient Kama Sutra?"

"I think the Kama Sutra is already the ancient Kama Sutra." This time, Ash rewarded his sass by punching him in the shoulder. He pretended like it didn't hurt. "Judy said it was supposed to bring good luck to a newlywedded couple. These must be how you trigger the blessing."

"*Blessing*, really?"

"Gimme a break. It says 'be blessed,' okay?" Sam trailed his fingers over the flowing script. The back of the canvas was coarse, but the trails of ink were smooth to the touch. "I think it's a translation of whatever this other language is. It's in a similar format, see?"

"Whatever. That's not important."

"Okay, what is important then?"

"Deciding where I'm going to put it."

Ash took the painting from him and walked to the bookshelf facing the bed, setting it on the second-to-highest shelf. Standing back to admire her work, she nodded.

"That'll do until I can get the stud finder and mount it on the wall." She turned, grinning like a fool. "Whoever HPL is was one dramatic bitch. I love it!"

9

Brian Murray stumbled over the curb, nearly dropping the bottle of bottom-shelf vodka. Through luck, or perhaps the grace and agility only the staggeringly drunk could manage, he was able to both stay upright and keep hold of the bottle.

His worn boots scuffed against the macadam as he stumbled into the dark alley. His alley. Brian had been living in it for the better part of three months—the longest he had stayed in any place since he'd gotten out of jail two years earlier. The alley wasn't much, but its narrow walls kept the worst of the biting wind off him, and only one of the adjacent buildings was open for business, so there was very light foot traffic. The other businesses in the small shopping mall Brian called temporary home, a knitting store and a thrift shop, were shuttered for the evening.

It had been a long day, and he wanted nothing more than to crawl into bed and sleep until the inevitable thirst came over him again. Memories of the day slogged through the morass of his mind, causing him to chuckle. His breath was so laden with fumes it could peel paint.

Long day, but *good*.

He collected enough money to not only buy two bottles of good booze—"good" being loosely applied—but to also to buy the company of a lady—"lady" also being loosely applied. It'd been far too long since he'd been with a woman. Longer than Brian wanted to admit even to himself.

The trip from the mouth of the alley seemed longer than usual that night, but he finally made it home. A small fort constructed of flattened cardboard boxes, milk crates, and empty pallets.

On his hands and knees, he scuttled through the entrance curtained by a ratty old tarp he found in the dumpster. Propping himself on a pillow of flattened boxes, he drained the rest of the bottle. The vodka that didn't end up in his beard flowed down his gullet and mixed pleasantly with the stew he'd eaten earlier.

A damn good day.

Brian pulled an assortment of coats and sweaters over himself. The same place he'd gotten the stew, the church on All Saints Street, distributed the coats, and he grabbed extra for just this purpose.

A flash of annoyance threatened to disrupt his contentment. He was grateful for the food and coats, but he could do without all the Bible-thumping he was subjected to at the church.

If it even was the Bible they were thumpin'. He didn't pay close enough attention to know what kind of church it was. It seemed like they were always changing, anyways, so how could he keep up with it all? Though, it could have been his state of mind whenever he visited...

Whatever the case, he could do without the constant offers of salvation. Some of his fellows on the streets took them up on their offer, and Brian never saw them again. He liked to think they got their lives together and moved on, but rumors abounded. Telling stories was one

THE ACCURSED

of their few pastimes, so there were some whoppers out there. Despite the pleasant warmth radiating from his belly, a shiver coursed through him.

A burp burbled its way up his throat, and he settled down into the pile of coats. Sleep came quickly. Two bottles of booze and an empty nutsack would do that to a man. The rip-roaring sound of his snoring rattled the lean-to within moments of his eyes shutting.

Ordinarily, the unseasonably warm evening and the stomach full of booze would let him sleep all night and wake up…if not rested then at least not feeling like the gum stuck underneath a bus stop bench.

But not that night.

Moments after his eyes closed, dark tendrils pushed up from the detritus of Brian's nest. In the dark, it was impossible to discern color or any other detail. The alley was too narrow to catch the moon's rays, and there were no streetlamps in that part of town.

The tendrils writhed ever closer toward the sleeping man like a weed seeking a source of water.

The thin veins brushed against his skin, and Brian giggled. In his vodka-soaked dreaming, it wasn't pulsing black follicles caressing him but the hands of a certain overly perfumed companion.

As soon as the tendrils touched his skin, they wriggled faster, as a puppy does when it sees its dinner bowl. The thin tentacles slipped under Brian's clothes and across his flesh, splitting off fresh shoots like tree roots, their touch as gentle as a whisper.

Within moments, Brian's body was crisscrossed by the black filaments. The things ceased their motion, the only sound in the alley Brian's deep, steady breathing.

Then his screams shattered the silence.

Dark tendrils burrowed into his skin, delving deep to find the water and nutrients within. Brian's shriek was loud and shrill, but it lasted only a moment. The wriggling vines around his chest constricted, and the air in his lungs gushed out like a bellows. The vines ratcheted down farther, and the last breath Brian took ended in a whimper.

Brian would suffocate in mere moments. His extremities would go numb, and soon after, his brain would shut down as he slipped into unconsciousness, then death. Unfortunately, the tendrils didn't let Brian's consciousness slip into death's numb embrace.

They tasted blood, and they wanted more.

The hideous veins pulsed as they sucked liquid life out of the homeless man's body. They shuddered and throbbed with each slowing beat of his heart. Deeper, they burrowed, seeking the heat and the organs that housed Brian's delicious life force. The snaking tendrils found his heart, then, like a root forcing its way through a sidewalk, they cracked his skull and tunneled into his brain.

By then, Brian welcomed oblivion.

10

"Mornin', Sam."

"Good morning, Mr. Williams."

Mr. Williams' gaze was steely over the top of the newspaper. "Would it kill you to call me Bruce for once? I think we've known each other long enough to give up the formality." Sam pursed his lips, considering the ramifications and potential repercussions of such an event. Ash called his mom Alice, after all, and the man had basically been his surrogate father for over ten years…

"I wouldn't want to risk it, Mr. Williams."

The older man shook his head and returned to the paper, but not before Sam caught the grin pulling at the corner of his mouth.

"Tragic news today," he said a moment later.

"What's up?"

Mr. Williams' voice was somber from the other side of the paper. "English teacher up at the high school is in a coma."

A pang of concern jolted through Sam. "Oh man, was it Mr. Pinkett?"

"Ms. Cornell. You know her?"

"She teaches freshman English. She started when we were sophomores, so we never had her." Relief flooded through him that one of his favorite teachers wasn't hurt, guilt hot on its heels that he was relieved someone else was in a coma. "Do they know what happened?"

He was silent for a minute, his eyes scanning the article. "Her adult daughter found her late yesterday afternoon, asleep in a chair. When she couldn't wake her up, she called 9-1-1." He folded the paper and set it on the table beside his plate. "Doesn't say what happened. Just that she's stable."

Ash's heavy footsteps sounded on the stairs. "Morning, Pop." She strolled into the kitchen and poured herself a box of Frosted Flutes.

"Mornin', pumpkin." He tipped a large thermos of steaming coffee down his gullet and did a double-take, nearly choking on it. When he finally caught his breath, he exclaimed, "You're dressed!"

Ash was sporting a miniskirt and a top that said *Nip & Suck It*, a gray hoodie zipped over it. "Um, yeah. They kinda frown at going to school naked."

"You know what I mean." His eyes bounced to Sam and back. "You're not prancing around in your underwear."

Sam pulled the paper over and glued his eyes to the story about Ms. Cornell, his ears pinking. Usually, Sam didn't notice what Ash was wearing, whether she was prancing around in her undies and a baggy shirt or a skintight miniskirt that drew attention to her ass like his eyes were magnets.

That morning, he spotted her outfit as soon as she walked into the kitchen. All he could think about, even as he scanned the article about the teacher's tragic accident, was how badly he wanted to see her in her panties again, disheveled hair all mussed up from sleeping. He shook his head and forced his attention to the newspaper article.

Stupid, traitorous hormones...

"First off, I've never pranced anywhere. Second, Randy will be here in a few minutes to pick me up." Through an overflowing bite of Frosted Flutes, she said to Sam, "I thought I texted you he was giving me a ride?"

"Nope, but it's no big deal." If Randy was about to show up he wanted to get out of there. He saw enough of the guy already. Unfortunately, standing up right then was a non-starter. If he did, he'd give everyone a front-row seat to what was going on in his pants.

It's like puberty all over again!

Ash brushed past him, balancing the almost overflowing bowl. "Grab some grub before you go. You know how Dad gets if he doesn't get to feed anyone for a while."

"No, it's fine, really."

"C'mon, Sammy. I made breakfast pizza." Bruce jumped to his feet and hurried into the kitchen. He really did love cooking for people, and with Ash's busy social life, he didn't get the chance that often. A steaming casserole dish emerged from the oven, and the aroma of sausage and potatoes blanketed the room.

Ash disappeared upstairs, and a few minutes later, her footsteps descended the steps again. "Bye, Pops. Love ya!"

"Ashley Williams, I know you didn't leave that bowl in your room!" The sound of the door slamming was the only response. Shaking his head, he placed a plate heaping with layers of Pillsbury pie crust, cheese, sausage, and potato in front of Sam. He dropped a similarly laden plate on the other side of the table and then two cups filled with orange juice.

"Thanks, Mr. Williams. This smells great."

The man nodded through a bite of the piping hot casserole. He wiped a stream of grease from his chin. "Everything okay with you and Ash?"

Sam's fork paused halfway to his mouth. Memories of last night flitted through his head like a highlight reel of his most embarrassing moments. "What do you mean?"

Bruce swallowed a long drink of coffee. He'd save the orange juice for last, as usual. "She's been dating that...*boy* all school year, and I can only think of a couple times he's driven her to school." The words "that boy" came out of his mouth like he was chewing on broken glass.

Unbidden, images flash through Sam's mind. Ash sitting astride him, her knees pinning his arms down. How her breasts pressed against his chest, the warm taste of her lips on his.

And then some not-so-great memories. How he had to hide his raging boner behind that stupid painting. How she noticed him checking her out in her pajamas. How she wrapped herself around that pillow like she was using it as a shield.

"Um, yeah. Everything's fine. I think she just wants to spend time with Randy before he leaves for Spring Break."

Mr. Williams finished his breakfast, looking for all the world like he was being forced to eat manure. The food was too hot by half for Sam, but he scarfed it down regardless. A burnt tongue was a cheap price to pay to get out of answering more questions.

"Let your mom know I'll be around tomorrow morning sometime to take a look at that leaky faucet."

THE ACCURSED

"Will do. Thanks, Mr. Williams."

Sam and Ash didn't normally hang out much at school. They had their own cliques, which were drastically different from each other's. They chatted in between classes, and in the one class they shared—third period Econ—they sat next to each other, but most of their interaction at school was via text.

When Sam got to school, he saw Randy's car in the parking lot, but he didn't see either of them before the bell rang for first period. Normally, he'd run into Ash on her way from second to third period, but he didn't he didn't see her then, either.

Randy was in second period, though, which wasn't weird in itself. The really weird thing was that Randy was there *before* the bell rang. It was also strange that he looked like he'd just rolled out of bed. Randy was many things—douchebag, vapid socialite, spoiled rich boy—but one thing he wasn't was messy. He was always put together. Clothes, hair, everything in immaculate order. Today, however, he was a mess. Rumpled clothes and dry, disheveled hair. Not wet like it normally was after his post-workout shower. Despite that, a shit-eating grin split his face nearly in two.

Sam didn't try to hide the surprise on his face as he slipped into his desk. He opened his mouth to ask Randy where Ash was, but the bell rang, and Mr. Pinkett started talking.

Sam wasn't the only one who noticed the change in Randy's appearance. Veronica twisted in her seat the first chance she got. "What happened to you? You look like you just got your d—" she cut her words off with a glance toward the front of the room. "Like the cat who caught the canary."

Scott's brows furrowed, and his gaze bounced from Veronica to Randy and back. Finally, his eyes lit up with a dawning epiphany. Probably the first epiphany he'd ever experienced. "Daaaamn, bro. Did you finally tap that?"

Before Randy could respond, Mr. Pinkett interrupted, "Anything you'd like to share with the class?" The three students fell silent and turned their attention to the teacher.

Sam's stomach dropped, and he looked at Randy from the corner of his eye. Was Veronica right? Did Ash finally let Randy take her to the old locker room?

God, he hoped not.

Not just because he despised Randy. Not just because Sam hadn't been able to stop thinking about her since she'd kissed him. But because he knew Ash wasn't ready to lose her virginity. She talked about it *all the time*, so Sam was well aware how nervous she was to go past third base with Randy.

The idea of her fucking Randy was bad enough. But Sam had to wonder if somehow *he* was responsible for the turn of events. The idea of her fucking Randy because of something he did made him sick to his stomach. He remembered her expression when Sam ogled her, how she'd hid behind the pillow.

She came downstairs today fully dressed. That she was ready that early was a miracle. And then she'd asked Randy to pick take her to school. Was it all a coincidence, or had his attention skeeved her out?

It was bad enough dredging up all these feelings that he thought he'd killed and buried. But if he was somehow responsible for her and Randy finally hooking up...he didn't know how he could handle that.

His long-buried feelings were resurfacing like some kind of zombie. His lecherous attention could have repulsed his best friend. Not only that, but it could have been the reason she finally slept with Randy.

Everything is coming apart.

This was exactly why he'd tried so hard to bury these feelings in the first place. When she started paying attention to other boys and made it clear she wasn't interested in him romantically, he knew he had to do something to maintain their friendship. Ash was basically family, and he wasn't going to let his unrequited feelings drive someone else out of his life.

He needed to fix this. But how?

11

"I'll take it from here, Mr. Dyer. Why don't you just follow along silently?"

After Sam read the same line of dialog four times in a row, Mr. Pinkett took over reading the part of Professor Drake. As embarrassed as he was for flubbing the lines, he was grateful to Mr. Pinkett. Too many thoughts were whirling through Sam's head for him to focus. Plus, the bright-eyed, square-jawed, broad-shouldered teacher was a much better analog for the dashing Professor Drake. The dreamy expressions of Sam's female classmates were evidence enough of that. Unlike them, Sam wasn't enraptured with the teacher's performance, belted out with gusto in his sonorous baritone.

What the hell am I going to do?

The rest of English class passed in a fog. Every time he tried to sort through his feelings for Ash, the implications overwhelmed him.

They'd been friends since childhood, since before kindergarten. There was a time—when he was six—when he'd tell anyone who listened that he was going to marry Ashley Williams. But any notion of marriage, or any kind of romance, with Ash dried up a long time ago.

Or did they? He thought he'd moved on, but what if he was just fooling himself this whole time? And if he did like her, should he tell her? He almost laughed aloud at that. He'd had a crush on Veronica Chambers since the start of high school and barely mustered the courage to sit next to her in class.

"Earth to Sam."

The words yanked him out of his personal vortex of worries. Veronica was twisted in her seat, looking like she was waiting for an answer.

"Sorry, what?"

She shared an amused expression with April Sullivan in the row beside her. "I asked if you were excited for the Spring Fling Dance."

The freight train of Sam's thoughts lurched off its tracks. "What? Oh, um, yeah. I guess."

"Do you have a date yet?"

"Me?" He was laughing before he could stop himself. Veronica cocked her head, a small frown on her face. Sam quelled the incredulous laughter and straightened his face. "Nope, I don't."

She stared at him silently for a moment longer. "Yeah, me neither."

Her eyes bored into him, and the silence grew.

Do I have breakfast on my face?

"I'm sure you won't have a problem getting one." With a small smile and nod, he turned his attention back to the play. The class wasn't reading aloud anymore, so they must be reading on their own. His mind was anywhere but on the words in front of him. Veronica grunted and turned to face the front again.

The bell rang a few minutes later, and everyone jumped up to escape W.R. Mann's gothic tale of romance and woe.

THE ACCURSED

Sam's lingering thoughts slowed him down, and he was one of the last to gather his stuff. Veronica threw him a sharp glance and stormed out of class. She was wearing heavy combat boots, so if she was going for a dramatic exit, she nailed it.

What the hell is that all about? Confused, he tracked her shadow against the window blinds as she descended the walkway. It wasn't until the silhouette disappeared and he was left alone in the room that his mind ran through their conversation.

Holy shit, was she fishing for a date to the dance? If Ash were here, this was the time that she'd hit him, probably with an annoyed "Duh!" for good measure. With a sinking feeling, he remembered what Ash had told him. Veronica thought he was cute.

He looked down at the clothes Ash bought for him. A pair of dark jeans, tighter than he preferred but not so tight that it was obscene, and a light blue polo shirt. He wasn't sure what he thought about the ensemble, but if the new outfit had anything to do with why Veronica chose that day to talk to him, then it could be Ash actually knew what she was doing.

Should I go after her? His knees almost buckled at the thought. *On second thought, now probably isn't the best time.* He *had* just pissed her off. Best to let her cool down. The dance wasn't until the Friday after Spring Break, so there was plenty of time.

Ash's desk in third period remained empty. Where the hell was she? *I hope everything's okay.* It wasn't like her to miss class. She wasn't a committed student by any means, but she didn't normally ditch. Well, she wouldn't ditch by herself, at least. And he, Randy, and Gwen were still at school.

So where the hell is she? He checked his phone again, but she still hadn't responded to his texts.

In the passing period between fifth and sixth periods, Sam approached Gwen. Gwen was a snob and never passed up an opportunity to sneer at him, but if something was going on with Ash then Gwen would know.

"Have you seen Ash today?"

Gwen and Amber turned around, matching scowls on their faces. He could almost feel their gazes dropping and climbing up his body. Fighting the urge to hide behind his backpack, he repeated the question.

The girls blinked like a beam of light strafed across their eyes.

Gwen chewed ponderously, smacking her lips and blowing a large pink bubble with her gum. It popped and with a swipe of her tongue the gum disappeared back into her mouth.

"Yeah. Earlier. Why?"

"Do you know where she is now?"

The two girls shared a glance, having a silent conversation Sam couldn't even guess at. The girls came to a silent arrangement, and two pairs of eyes pierced him.

Another bubble popped. "I like your new look."

Sam squirmed, and all of a sudden, the shirt felt too tight. "Um...thanks, I guess. So...do you know where Ash is?"

Her gaze lingered on him a moment longer. "Sure. I can take you to her."

"That's okay, you can just tell me."

THE ACCURSED

She shrugged, and the hem of her already short shirt rose to expose a flat stomach. He didn't realize he was staring until she turned away from him.

"Math is for suckers, anyways. C'mon." Amber gestured for him to go ahead of her, and with a shrug, he reluctantly followed Gwen.

He scanned the crowd of milling students, looking for Ash's familiar form, but his gaze kept straying back to Gwen's swaying hips. She was a petite girl and didn't have much going on in the trunk, but she worked what she had. With half his mind searching for Ash and the other half trying not to look at Gwen, he wasn't paying attention to their path.

"Have you ever been in the old locker room?"

Sam's feet tangled, and he stumbled. Regaining his balance, his eyes widened when he realized where they were heading. The old locker room loomed in the distance on the far side of the soccer field. Between them and the dilapidated brick building, dozens of lower-classmen mingled on blacktop basketball courts.

The ability to speak eluded him until he swallowed the lump in his throat. "Why? Is that where Ash is?" His stomach soured. Every guy in school fantasized about visiting the old locker room and getting an Elsbury High welcome, but the last thing he wanted was to see Ash in there with Randy.

A matching predatory grin stretched across Gwen and Amber's lips. Gwen laughed like he'd told a joke. As Gwen resumed walking, Amber tugged on his arm. "Come on." They walked arm-in-arm for a few strides, then she pushed him ahead of her.

With each step, the part-blue-mostly-rusted door of the locker came into view. That part of campus was neglected and almost looked like undeveloped forest. The building had practically been swallowed by the ancient red oaks surrounding it, their vestigial leaves still pale this time of year.

Why do I get the feeling I'm being led to the gallows?

His mind raced. He wanted to find Ash and learn what was going on with her; he couldn't shake the instinct that something bad had happened. Then again, he may just be overreacting to her ditching him for Randy that morning. It wasn't like he'd been in the best frame of mind since…since what happened the previous night, so chances were everything was fine.

As clueless as Sam was, even he wasn't so blind not to realize that Gwen and Amber weren't taking him to see Ash. Part of him was okay with that—more than okay, if he was being honest. Gwen and Amber were *really hot*. Amber may have been dumber than a sack of cats, but it wasn't her ability to recite the Quadratic Equation that was making his new jeans tighten. His wide eyes moved from the quickly approaching locker room back to Gwen's swaying hips. He gulped loud enough the girls could probably hear it.

The drab brick building was only ten yards away when Sam snapped out of it. Even if he wasn't worried about Ash, he was pretty sure Veronica wanted him to ask her to the spring fling dance. If she found out he messed around with Gwen and Amber, his chances with her might be over before things even began.

It took a monumental effort to change his course like inertia—or a cocktail of thirsty teenage hormones—was pulling him along in Gwen's wake. Almost like they didn't want to, his eyes stayed glued to Gwen's ass until the last nanosecond.

He forgot about Amber.

"Whoops," she said in an unconvincing tone. She stumbled and fell against him, pressing her chest against him. Her hands slid down his torso like she was trying to catch herself. The tips of her fingers curl around the waistband of his jeans, and she turned her icy blue eyes on him. "I'm *so* clumsy. Good thing you were here to catch me." She ran her fingertips along the inside of his waistband, tickling the hairs on his abdomen, that predatory grin back on her face.

"Um, sorry," he said, pushing her away gently. Her bottom lip pouted, and she clung to his waistband for a moment longer before finally letting go.

"What's up?" Gwen called, leaning against the rusted door that led into the locker room.

"I just remembered I need to go to the quiz. I mean…retake a bathroom. No—um…" Sam juked around Amber. "Thanks for your help!"

Randy and Scott were at the flagpole, lounging on the concrete patio table like usual. Sam fidgeted, his eyes scanning the crowds, and he tried not to roll his eyes every time Scott's gaze tracked every girl that passed. Randy, at least, was more subtle about it, checking them out from the corner of his eye.

After the embarrassing debacle with Gwen and Amber, Sam hadn't had any luck finding Ash. It didn't help that he had to spend most of sixth period in the bathroom waiting for his erection to subside.

Something barreled into him and nearly knocked him over. Arms wrapped around his chest. His knee-jerk reaction was to throw an elbow into the person's head, thinking it was Randy or Scott, but a split second later, he smelled Ash's shampoo and recognized her auburn hair. She was sobbing.

"Holy shit, what's wrong?"

Randy noticed and strolled over. "What's wrong, babe?"

She tried talking, but a sob cut the words off. Sam pulled her into a tight hug. Randy awkwardly put a hand on her shoulder and stared daggers at Sam. Sam ignored him. "Are you okay? I've been looking for you all day."

Ash pulled out of the hug, sniffling. Her eyes were puffy, her cheeks blotchy. She hated crying in public and covered her face. "It's Ju-Ju-udy."

"What happened?"

"I was in the nurse's office, and Amanda Petrick came in sobbing her eyes out. Judy is in a coma!"

"Who's Judy?"

Sam shot Randy a withering glare, but the dudebro was immune to scorn. Ash started to cry again, and Sam hugged her until the tears stopped. A moment later, she sniffed and threw herself into Randy's arms. Somehow, he looked even more smug as he wrapped his arms around her.

A sour sick burbled in his stomach. "Tell me what happened."

Ash unburied her face, wiping her eyes on the sleeve of her sweater. "She didn't open the store this morning. The restaurant owner next door had a spare key, and when he went in, he found her in the back unconscious."

Randy's face scrunched up. "Wait, the lady who runs the thrift store? Why are you upset about that?"

THE ACCURSED

Ash yanked away from him. Sam couldn't see her face, but he could imagine her expression. "She's Amanda's grandma. And Judy's a friend, you jerk!"

Randy shot Sam a look and led her away, saying something low that Sam couldn't hear. Based on body language, their conversation wasn't a pleasant one.

Sam and Scott stood in silence. It was probably the only time the two had ever been alone with each other. Luckily, there wasn't enough time for things to get truly awkward. The hushed argument wound down. Randy reached for her hand, but Ash pulled away, her back ramrod straight as she approached Sam. "Will you give me a ride home?"

"Um, yeah. Of course." In silence, they walked to the Tercel, Sam doing his best to ignore Randy's glare. The two dudebros got into Randy's Mustang and peeled out of the parking lot.

There was a lot Sam wanted to say…to ask. Where Ash had been all day. About Randy, the old locker room, and if she'd decided to lose her virginity. But he couldn't bring himself to let the words out. In that moment, he realized he really didn't want to know.

"What happened with Judy?"

Out the passenger side window, Ash watched the houses and empty lots roll by. "They say it was a gas leak."

Sam parked in the Williams' driveway and pulled Ash into a hug. She squeezed him, silent sobs wracking her.

"It'll be okay. Judy will be fine. She's a tough old gal. I can't imagine something like a gas leak doing her in. She's too ornery for that."

Something like a phlegmy chuckle came from somewhere around his collarbone. She gave him one last squeeze and pulled away, wiping her eyes and nose with her sleeve. "'Ornery,' really? God, you sound like my dad."

"No, I sound like *his* dad." They laughed, and the gloom receded for the moment. "Come on, let's get you some tea."

Only family was able to visit Judy, so they spent the rest of the day together, watching movies and talking. Just like old times.

Old times, he thought. *Two days ago—before my body decided I still had the hots for my best friend.*

Ash held it together until she had to explain everything all over again when Mr. Williams got home. Tears streamed down her cheeks like she'd ripped open a fresh scab. Mr. Williams was one of the few people who understood Ash's relationship with Judy. Tears gathered in the older man's eyes. Sam wasn't surprised. Mr. Williams looked like a beast of a man, but he was a marshmallow and never afraid to show it.

Sam called his mom to let her know he was staying the night. She was shaken up at what happened to Judy, having already heard from a mutual friend. Alice Dyer had known Judy longer than Sam and Ash had been alive. He asked if she wanted him to come home, but she said he should stay with Ash.

Once upon a time when Sam slept over, he and Ash would sleep in the same bed. She had a queen-sized mattress, so it was plenty big, but sometime around puberty, through unspoken agreement, they'd stopped doing that. He now slept on the floor or on the oversized beanbag chair. He could have stayed in the guest room, but that would defeat the point of a sleepover. It was hard to gossip from 40 feet away. That night he opted for the beanbag chair, dragging it over so he was beside Ash's bed just in case she needed something during the night.

THE ACCURSED

It was quiet in the dark room after they settled down. Finally, Sam asked the question that'd been burning in his head. "Are you and Randy going to be okay?" In the dark, he closed his eyes and said a silent prayer that they broke up during the argument earlier. The last thing Ash needed right now was to go through a breakup, but *come on*, the guy was a major douchelord. Ash groaned, and Sam perked up.

That's a good sign, but then a moment later she dashed his hopes.

"Yeah, we're fine. I called him when you were in the shower and apologized."

"*You* apologized to *him*?"

She chuckled. "Yeah, go figure. Turns out I *am* capable of doing it."

Randy is the one who should apologize for being such a jerk. He didn't want to stir things up, so he stayed quiet. He fell silent, staring at the shadows the nightlight cast onto the ceiling. His eyes traced the shapes, finding images in the dark splotches the way a kid found animals in clouds. His eyes eventually landed on the bookshelf and the new painting. He remembered the inscription on the back. The blessing. Thoughts cavorted through his sleepy mind with abandon, making connections his fully awake consciousness would have ridiculed.

"Hey, maybe it was the blessing that caused Judy's coma." He chuckled at the ridiculous thought, then cut short his own mirth. He'd spoken without considering what Ash had gone through that day. As soon as he realized he'd made a joke about Judy's condition, his stomach clenched. To his surprise, Ash neither exploded into tears nor expletives.

Maybe she's already asleep.

Finally, Ash chuckled. "Yeah, that explains it."

With a lurch, his heart started beating again. Relief flooded him like he'd taken his first breath after holding it. Carefully, he continued down the line of thought his tired imagination cooked up. "It did say something about laying in death, right? Almost made it sound like a curse. First Ms. Cornell, and now Judy."

Ash yawned into the glooming darkness, and the bed springs squeaked beneath her. He could see her bright green eyes even in the dim nightlight. She spoke through a jaw-cracking yawn. "Yeah. Maybe tomorrow morning I'll head over to Randy's before he leaves town and bang him so the crazy artist lady's blessing doesn't turn into a curse and kill everyone."

Sam's blood ran cold, and it had nothing to do with the prospect of an evil curse ravaging the town. The whimsical musings of his sleepy brain were burned away like fog in the sunlight, and he came fully awake.

The weight and trials of the day took their toll on Ash, and she drifted asleep. She snored when on her back, and soon enough, a series of low grunts and whistles stuttered out of her nose.

Sam lay awake, staring at the shadows until sleep finally claimed him.

12

When Ash awoke the next morning, she and Sam were holding hands. As a child, she was prone to clutching something in her sleep. Usually, it was Mr. Dunderhead, an overstuffed, multicolored caterpillar she took everywhere with her. And if she was really scared, she'd crawl into bed with her parents and hold their hands.

She was too big to crawl into her dad's bed, and Mr. Dunderhead fell apart years ago. A mountain of pillows was all she had on her bed now. During nights when she was scared or sad, it was one of these she wrapped her whole body around, squeezing all comfort and support she could from it. It wasn't nearly as comforting as Mr. Dunderhead or being tucked warmly in her parent's bed, but it usually worked.

Last night, Sam scooted the beanbag close so he could be close by. Sometime in the night she must have reached down and grabbed his hand.

Ash raked the hair out of her face that came loose from her ponytail while she slept. Sam was one of those gross people who enjoyed getting up in the morning, so she was surprised he was still snoring quietly. Sleeping in the beanbag always made him snore, probably something to do with the awkward angle. A loud, guttering snort issued from his open mouth, and she buried her face into a pillow so he couldn't hear her laughing.

The blanket he started the night with lay crumpled in a heap on the floor. He was a hot sleeper, so he rarely ended the night with anything more than a sheet. His arms and legs sprawled off the beanbag like someone poured him onto it, wearing nothing but a pair of pajama bottoms he kept at her place. They'd slept at each other's houses so often each of them had spare clothes for the occasion, usually older stuff they didn't wear routinely.

He's such a doofus when he sleeps. She had to fight to keep in the laughter. His hair stuck up at all angles, and his mouth gaped like a fish. He looked like a baby bird waiting for its mama to feed it. All resemblance to a baby bird stopped there, though. He wasn't scrawny at all and clearly never skipped leg day. Sam had a deceptively hot body. He didn't flaunt it like most guys would, but he worked hard to maintain it.

He doesn't make a big deal about anything, she thought, shaking her head at her friend's hopelessness. *Especially if it means drawing attention to himself.* It was too bad he didn't try harder to be noticed. Some girl out there didn't know what she was missing underneath all that denim and flannel. Absently, her eyes lingered on Sam's sleeping form. His chest, the six-pack abs, the heart-bedecked pajamas that were a year too small for him.

"Oh god," she half-exclaimed and half-laughed, clamping her eyes closed and turning away. She knew it was normal—healthy even—for guys to get morning wood, but Sam's old pair of pajamas were a little too tight to hide what he had going on down there.

THE ACCURSED

His snore cut off mid-crescendo, grunting when the pillow she chucked took him squarely between the legs. "Oof! Wha—huh?" She hadn't meant to hit him there, but it was like trying not to stare at bright headlights when you're driving in the dark. Her gaze just kept gravitating in that direction...

She rolled off the other side of the bed and stretched, pretending like she'd just woken up. He grunted, then she turned to him when she heard him pull the blanket up.

"Good morning!"

"Why are you throwing pillows at me?"

"It must have fallen off the bed when I rolled over."

He gave her a look that said he didn't believe her, but he didn't press. "Hungry?"

"I could eat. Once my balls descend from my stomach, that is."

Ash slipped on a thick pair of socks and a baggy sweater. "Why do guys always talk about their balls?"

Sam levered himself out of the sunken recesses of the beanbag chair. The blanket fell, and he scrambled to catch it. Ash pretended not to notice.

"The better question is, why are girls always hitting us in the balls?"

"Just giving you an opportunity to talk about your favorite subject, I guess."

Sam searched the floor for his discarded clothes. "I'm gonna go to the bathroom." He walked sideways toward the door like he was trying to hide something from her sight.

"I'll meet you downstairs." When the bathroom door closed, she figured it was safe to venture out. She hoped to catch a whiff of something delicious coming from the kitchen, but she just smelled the lingering scent of black coffee. Wherever her dad went this morning, he'd left early.

Barkley yipped and bounded toward her from his favorite perch on the back of the couch. The pup usually woke when her dad did, but once he got his breakfast, he was happy to chill and wait for her to wake up. A few minutes later, Sam came down the stairs, looking much more comfortable in yesterday's clothes.

"Back to normal?" she asked before she could process it. She buried her head in the pantry to hide her mortified blush. *Jesus, Ash, stop thinking about it!*

The hesitation in his voice was evidence that he picked up on the awkward phrasing. "Uh, yeah. What's for breakfast?"

"I was hoping Dad made something, but it looks like he had an early job."

"He said something about checking out a leaky pipe for my mom. He probably went to my house."

"Checking her pipes, eh?" Ash bobbed her eyebrows. After Sam's dad and Ash's mom ran off together, they often joked that their remaining parents would get married and they'd all be one happy family again.

"Ew, gross." Sam exaggerated a shudder. "That'd be weird."

"What's weird about it?"

Sam's mouth opened a couple times before answering. "You know...old people sex." He pantomimed another whole-body shudder, then picked up the newspaper her dad left on the table.

She narrowed her eyes. Even with everything going on—Randy going to Atlantic City for Spring Break and Judy's accident—she had noticed that Sam was being weird.

THE ACCURSED

Weirder than normal, that is. He had been all week. Once she noticed something, Ash wasn't the type to beat around the bush. She opened her mouth to demand he tell her what was up but shut it with an audible click.

An image of this morning prowled through her mind. Sam in his too-small pajamas, covering himself with the blanket so she wouldn't see his...*condition*.

He's probably just embarrassed. She would be, too, if she were in his position.

Actually, that was a lie. It's a good thing she didn't have a dick 'cause she'd show it to literally *everyone*. She'd be sending dick pics like Oprah gave out mid-sized sedans. She laughed at the thought of the entertainment mogul blasting out dick pics, causing Sam to glance up from the paper.

"Sorry, don't mind me. Just losing my mind." She tossed hash brown patties into the oven and pulled out eggs and leftover bacon from the fridge. Sam didn't volunteer to help cook, but that was a good thing. The kid was good at just about everything he put his mind to, but cooking eluded him. The best he could do was toss a frozen pizza in the oven. From behind her, she heard the newspaper crinkle and fold.

A moment later, his hesitant voice broke the silence. "If someone liked someone, should they tell them?"

It was a good thing she wasn't looking at him otherwise he'd see her massive eye roll. "Yes, you should definitely tell Veronica you've got the hots for her." She took her attention away from the bubbling scrambled eggs long enough to catch the flush on his cheeks. She'd been down this road too many times with Sam, so she didn't get her hopes up that he'd actually do anything about it.

"I didn't say anything about Veronica."

"Mm-hmm."

He ignored her. "And what if the person is in a relationship? Would you still tell them?"

She fought to hold back the exasperated sigh. Why was he being so hedgy? They'd told each other everything since...well, since as long as she could remember.

"Not talking about stuff and keeping secrets are cheap plot devices for teen dramas. Plus, I'm pretty sure that rumor about Veronica and Fernando Alvarez isn't true, so you've got nothing to worry about." His dour expression did little to dim the beaming smile on her face. "*And*," she continued, "even if it is true, at least you know she puts out." *Not that there was ever any doubt about that.* She kept that thought to herself, though.

Sam fell silent, mulling over whatever moral dilemma pretzel he'd tied himself into. That boy was always making things so much more complicated than they needed to be. A few minutes later, she set two plates on the table. The hash browns were a crispy dark brown just how he liked them. Before she could take a bite, the phone rang. There was a stunned, silent moment where they looked at each other like idiots, then the phone rang again.

"Is that... Is that the landline?"

"Jesus, I haven't heard that sound in ages."

"I forgot we even had one." She followed the claxon wail of the ancient phone. "Hello?" She listened while the person on the other line spoke, then her heart dropped into her stomach. The phone fell from her hand and bounced off the floor.

"What's—"

"My dad's in the hospital." Tears blurred her vision, but she heard Sam jump to his feet.

"I'll drive."

13

She had always hated hospitals. Ever since she was a kid and got strep throat. The nurse said the swab wouldn't hurt, that it would only tickle the back of her throat, but she lied. It hadn't been just a tickle. It felt like she'd been stabbed in the throat. She had retched and thrown up all over the nurse's scrubs. And Ash *hated* throwing up.

Please don't leave me. Please, please, please.

She sat beside her dad and thought those words. Over and over.

Bruce Williams was a big man. But in that room, under those harsh, unforgiving fluorescent lights, he looked small, hollow.

It took all her strength to reach out and take his hand. She half-expected it to be cold. The last—and only—time she'd visited someone in the hospital the person's hand was frail and chilly. She had been ten, and her dad brought her to Arkham Memorial to say her farewells to a grandma she barely knew. The old lady looked like she was in her hundreds, though she was only 64. Ash couldn't remember seeing anyone so sick, so frail.

When she finally plucked up the courage to hold his hand, it was warm. There was still strength in it. Little victory that it was, relief flooded her.

On the other side of the bed, Sam's eyes were equally red and puffy. He hadn't hesitated to hold her dad's hand.

She sniffed and cleared her throat. "What happened?"

The doctor, silent up to that point, allowing them to come to terms with the situation in their own time, spoke in a quiet, sure tone. "He was at the Sandersons' giving an estimate, and he fell off the ladder. Jason said he wasn't that high up, but...it doesn't take a big fall."

"So he has a concussion or something?" Sam asked.

"That's one concern, and we're testing for that. He also has lacerations to his right shoulder, elbow, and hip."

Ash sniffed. "That doesn't sound too bad, right?"

The doctor looked uncomfortable like she didn't want to say something. Sam picked up on the same thing. "What is it?"

"I'm not a forensic pathologist, but your dad's injuries aren't consistent with someone who's taken a fall from that height."

"What do you mean?"

Now that she'd broached it, the doc looked more comfortable continuing. "When you fall, it's natural to try to stop yourself. You put out your hands, elbows, knees. And there will be corresponding injuries. Based on your father's injuries, it doesn't appear that tried to arrest his fall."

Ash's face scrunched up. "So, what does that mean?"

It was Sam who answered. "He was already unconscious when he fell."

The doctor nodded. "That's a possibility. Or he wasn't in a state of mind where he realized what was happening."

Ash didn't know why, but she started crying again. A moment later, Sam's arms are around her, and he held her until the tears passed.

THE ACCURSED

The doctor held out a small box of tissues that may as well have been sandpaper.

"So what happens next?"

"We continue to monitor and run tests. I've ordered an MRI, EKG, and a blood panel. We should have a better idea of what's going on once we get the results."

Sam's voice reverberated in her ear. "How long?"

The doctor shifted her feet, looking uncomfortable again. "We can draw the blood and do the EKG, but the only MRI we have access to is in Dunwich. It's Saturday, so we're waiting to see if they can call in a radiologist."

"And if not?"

"Then we have to wait until Monday." Ash opened her mouth to protest, but the doc held up a hand. "I know it's frustrating. You want to know what's going on, and any amount of waiting is too much. We have to send out the blood panel anyway, and the lab is closed on weekends, so the earliest we can get results is Tuesday."

Ash nodded and turned back to the hospital bed, tears stinging her eyes. Sam and the doctor spoke some more, then she left. The only sounds in the room were the various beeps of the machines and the low hiss of the HVAC unit. Ash shivered. Hospitals were always too cold. A moment later, warmth enveloped her. Sam's flannel was large and warm and smelled safe. He snugged it tight against her and brushed a loose strand of her hair out of her face that had come loose.

"Do you need anything?" She shook her head. "I asked the doctor to send in some food since you haven't eaten yet."

"I thought the food was only for patients."

Sam shrugged. "I got the feeling she wanted to do *something* since all they can do is wait at this point."

"Naturally, you thought of food."

"Naturally." They shared a smile.

Sam slid his hands into his pant pockets and snugged his arms close to his body. Goosebumps rose along his forearms.

"Do you want your flannel back?"

"I'm fine. Thanks."

"You're not fine. I can see your nips through your shirt!"

Sam wrapped his arm around his chest, a scandalized expression on his face. She laughed, then noticed what he was wearing. "Hey, you're wearing the outfit I got you!"

They had to be the same clothes he wore yesterday since he hadn't left any of the new clothes at her place. A periwinkle polo over a pair of slim, tapered jeans. She would have bought skinny jeans if she thought he'd go for it, but there was no way he was ready for that.

The blue shirt really makes the gold in his eyes pop. Sam's dark blue eyes were flecked with an orange, almost golden color. *Not that anyone could see them through that tangle of hair.*

Sam plucked at the hem of the polo shirt self-consciously.

"Stop it. It looks fine. Now, turn around and show me the goods." She needled him until he relented and twirled for her. "See, I *told* you I knew what I was doing. I'd totally tap that."

Sam rolled his eyes, but he bit his lip to hold in laughter. He opened his mouth to say something—no doubt something snarky—but her dad chose that moment to let out a loud breath. Their heads jerked to look at him. She knew nothing about the machines hooked up to him, but as near as she could tell, there weren't any alarms going off. After the loud gasp, Dad continued to breathe, his heart monitor beeping its lively tune. She squeezed her eyes closed, but no more tears would come. She'd cried more in the last 24 hours than she had since her mother left.

"Do you..." Sam looked as uncomfortable as the doctor had when she was delivering bad news. Ash waited for him to continue, but after a second, he shook his head.

"What?"

"It's nothing."

"No really, what is it?"

He started and stopped again, then finally spat out whatever he'd been trying not to say. "Do you think—I know this is ridiculous—but...do you think that...the curse...could have something to do with all this?"

Ash's face scrunched, and she must be looking at him like he was growing a tit out of his forehead because he looked concerned. "What the fuck? What curse?"

"You know, on the Swedish fertility painting...thing."

Her gaze fell onto her dad's unconscious form, watching his chest rise and fall. "I don't want to talk about this."

"It's just that first, it was Ms. Cornell, then Judy. Now your dad."

"I said I don't want to talk about it."

Sam continued like he didn't hear her. "It's a pretty big coincidence that it all started the day after we...um..." Sam's eyes bulged like he was trying to hack up a furball. "...After you bought the painting. Right?"

"Stop it, Sam!" She glanced at the door, expecting a nurse to barge in and tell them to keep it down. "Now's not the time for whatever...whatever *this* is. Got it?"

Sam nodded and wisely didn't bring it up again. "Hey, how about I go grab us some coffee? It's gotta be terrible in a place like this, but it's something, right?"

"Why don't you just go home?" She probably said it more harshly than she intended, but she couldn't think about Sam's feelings at that moment.

Please don't leave me. Please, please, please. Over and over again.

She didn't have any other family. She didn't know where her mom was, so she couldn't even contact her. Not that she wanted to.

"Um...okay. I'll see you later?" Ash didn't reply as Sam walked to the door. "I'll swing by your house and pick up Barkley. He can stay with me and Mom until..." his voice trailed off. He stood silently for a minute, and when she didn't respond, he left.

14

THE WATER GUSHING OUT of the showerhead almost burned off a layer of her skin. Veronica snatched her hand away and dialed down the heat before stepping in, almost wishing she could do the same to the pressure. Almost, but not quite. Anything was better than the water pressure she had at home. She was lucky if the hot water lasted through even a quick shower. Something told her she didn't have to worry about running out of hot water here. The walk-in shower was all stone, one of those fancy ones that didn't even have a door or curtain, just a sloped tiled floor that funneled water down the drain.

This place is nice. Actually, everything of theirs was nice. Nice cars. Nice clothes.

Too bad their son doesn't stack up.

Nando was as clean-cut as they came. Straight A's. Sharply parted hair. A mouthful of perfect teeth—bought and paid for by mommy and daddy, of course. Went to mass every Sunday. An altar boy at St. Athammaus.

If she was honest, the goody-two-shoes act was the primary reason she set her sights on him. Looks-wise he wasn't anything to go wild about. When he went off to college—Ivy League, no doubt, following in his parents' footsteps—he wouldn't be the panty-dropper of the frat. His idea of foreplay was a little over-the-bra action. When she'd gone down on him, he'd popped before she even got a mouthful.

Not that he's even packing a mouthful.

Nando had two things going for him, that was, aside from the clean bed, money, and gloriously hot shower. He recovered quickly, and he was a skilled linguist. No, really. The guy could speak five languages.

It just so happened that one of those five languages was pussy because the guy ate her out like it was his job.

She fiddled with the temperature once more and then fully stepped into the current. Fog filled the spacious bathroom, the hot water on cold stone causing a considerable amount of steam.

Above the pluming cloud of mist, obfuscated by the wafting vapors, a thin black tendril snaked along the ceiling ever closer to the shower's occupant.

Veronica's skin pinked almost instantly, but she was going to enjoy the heat while she had it. She always had the urge to shower after sex. It wasn't any Freudian compulsion to wash her sins away or anything like that. People called her a slut, but she wasn't ashamed that she took charge of her sexual fulfillment. It just so happened that fulfillment for her meant a series of partners.

Monogamy was overrated. People didn't eat the same meal day after day. Why should dick be any different?

She showered after sex because she wanted to be clean. Women got a raw deal having to be humanity's cum catchers. If it wasn't in their snatches, it was in their mouths, on their tits, or on their faces. She didn't understand how guys could just lay around after sex stewing in the post-coital soup. It was probably some macho bullshit, the stench of their sex some kind of Neanderthal trophy-displaying ritual.

The thought made her skin crawl, and she shivered despite the water's heat. It was more than just the thought of Nando lying in bed covered in sweat and worse. This bathroom was unnaturally large. With the dim lights, thick clouds of steam, and the stone tiles echoing every sound, it was like she was in a cave. Or entombed. Another quiver skittered up her spine, and she quickened her pace.

The shower had three heads. One in the regular place, one in the ceiling large as a family-sized pizza, and a detachable head on a long hose. It took a minute to figure out how to make the detachable nozzle spray, but when she did, she set it to stun and blasted away every last bit of Fernando Alvarez from all her nooks and crannies.

In contrast to the elegance of the bathroom, Nando's soap of choice was a large bottle of Battleaxe 3-in-1 shower gel. She never had the urge to smell like medieval weaponry, but that was what you got when you hooked up with teenage guys still firmly ensconced in their man-child phase. With a sigh that somehow communicated all her angst, frustrations, and disappointments with the male of the species, Veronica squirted out a blob of foul-smelling goo that looked more like a sparkly booger than soap and began to wash herself.

A scraping sound caught her attention. "Nando, is that you?"

She brushed a few damp strands of hair out of her eyes and peered through the thickening fog. The sound like a bare foot sliding against tile floor shushed through the room. The bathroom was starting to give her the creeps. She considered calling for Nando and inviting him in with her. The last thing she wanted was another romp, but she would have welcomed the company if not his advances.

Directly above the shower, the black vine crawled down the walls toward the naked beauty, one filament finding the showerhead's pipe and coiling along its length, inching out over Veronica's head.

Closing her eyes, Veronica let the water run over her face, careful not to get her hair wet. She didn't have time to deal with that whole process. The hot water pounded against her face, and she turned off the flow to the detachable wand, placing it back on its cradle.

Her thumb brushed the rough surface of a thin tentacle, but its coarse flesh felt rough like a loofa, and she didn't think twice about it. Her hand was gone before it could grasp her finger.

The flow of water shut off with a trumpeting cry, the high pressure turning the pipes into an orchestra's brass section. Veronica ran her hands over her body, sluicing the water off, and then wrapped herself in a towel. The ever-present steam redoubled its efforts to blanket the room in dense fog. Luckily, the bathroom was spacious enough she didn't worry about tripping on anything while she picked her way toward the door.

As if realizing its quarry was about to escape, the vines lunged toward her, but the nude girl was too quick. For a moment, the roots act as if irked, shaking in the air like a frustrated politician wrung his hands. The moment passed, and the grasping vines in the shower settle into motionlessness like a trapdoor spider lying in wait for its prey to make a fatal misstep.

As the tendrils in the shower settled, those on the ceiling bulged and split, new shoots erupting and beginning the pursuit anew. The creeping, crawling things made a beeline for the door.

THE ACCURSED

Veronica, wrapped in a towel large enough to be a small blanket, slipped through the door and back into Nando's room, oblivious to the fate she narrowly avoided.

Nando's bedroom wasn't like any other room in the house that she'd seen. No ornate crown molding, no rich Merlot drapes adorning the windows. It looked just like any other teenage boy's room...if that boy grew up rich and sexually repressed. The furniture all matched. The floor was some kind of wood she didn't recognize. Maple? Walnut, possibly? A desktop computer lit with multicolored LEDs, at least two laptops, more gaming systems than she could name. But no pictures of scantily clad women. No Sports Illustrated magazines. Not even a hotrod calendar with babes in suggestive positions.

She had been in a lot of guys' rooms, but Nando's looked like it belonged to a bachelor in his 30s. Clean, tastefully decorated, and full of gadgets.

It must suck to be Catholic. She had friends who were Catholic. Christmas mass. Lent. Confession. Her grandma called them "good-time Catholics." But Nando's parents were like, *seriously* Catholic.

"Hey, sexy." Nando paused whatever he was watching, the dim light from the TV the only illumination aside from the weak moonlight slipping through the window. As expected, he was still lying in bed. By the expanse of skin she could see, he was still naked under the rumpled silk sheets. Nando smiled and stretched, the sheets sliding down to expose his shapeless stomach, revealing a mass of dark, manscaped hair. "No need to rush. Why don't you stay, and we can see how long this party can last?"

Veronica spotted her discarded clothes in a pile near the closet. "No thanks. I don't have time, even for a party that'll only last fifteen to thirty seconds." Despite the shadows cast over him, she saw the scowl slide over his face. She hooked her toes into the pile of clothes and kicked them up.

If it weren't so dark, and if she had been looking, she'd have seen the root under the heap, wriggling toward her.

Walking to the chair in the corner, she dropped the clothes in a pile and sorted through to find her bra and panties.

"Don't get me wrong, Nando. When it comes to oral, you've got game for days, but when it comes to laying the pipe..." She scrunched up her face and shrugged one shoulder. "I know it's a sin, but maybe spend a little more time cranking it. Do you mind?" Taking his scowl as all the answer she'd get, she shrugged out of the towel and slipped her undies on.

Might as well give the poor guy something for his spank bank.

Nodes formed on the pulsing dark vines, and new offshoots sprouted. Then more nodes and more offshoots. Soon, every wall in the room was crawling with the skittering things. Some crawled toward the dressing girl. Some wriggled their way along the wall toward the bed and the blushing boy atop it. Anger and lust heated his blood to an irresistible temperature. Still others raced for the door.

Nando's face flushed with scarlet indignation, and he jerked upright in bed, the sheet falling away completely. "You fucking slut, you think you're better than me?"

Classic fragile male ego. She almost laughed. "In bed? Yes." She popped her head out of the top of her blouse and gave him a cheeky smile.

THE ACCURSED

Her dimples did little to diffuse his anger. "I'm gonna tell everyone what you did."

"And what would that be? Give you the best sex of your life?"

"No! The other stuff—"

She cut him off. "Listen, Nando, I'm gonna stop you right there. First, *I'm* not ashamed of who *I* am. I am a little mortified that I jumped in *your* bed, but I take life by the balls and squeeze it for all it's worth. If there's a person in school who doesn't think I'm a slut, they're either an idiot or woefully naïve. *I* have no problems taking ownership of my actions. Which brings me to my second point..." She wriggled the skirt up her thighs, over her hips, then scooped up her shoes. Sauntering toward the bed, she leaned over the naked boy, a lewd smile plastered on her face.

A dopey smile grew on his round face, and she noticed his growing excitement.

Boys are so fucking dumb.

Her voice purred, deep and throaty. "*You,* on the other hand...you like to pretend you're this little goody-two-shoes. I wonder what your parents would think about what you did to me tonight?" The blood drained out of his face and dick like she'd slit his throat.

"I wonder what Maria Ortega would think. Haven't you two been promised to each other or some bullshit since the seventh grade? Isn't that ring on your finger supposed to represent chastity?"

Veronica chuckled and slipped her shoes on. As she walked to the door, she shot Nando double finger guns, stepping over the grasping tendrils without noticing. "Don't worry, though. I'll keep your secret. The last thing I want is to get that tongue locked down. You've got a gift, Nando. It'd be a shame if your 'rents shipped you off to seminary."

Her back bumped against the door, and her hand found the knob, not realizing that no matter how hard she pulled, the door wouldn't budge. A web of veins crisscross the portal, locking it in place, the black filaments nearly invisible in the dark room.

"Toodles," she said, giving him a jaunty wave.

"Wait!"

"I know you Catholics are into shame and flagellation, but this"—she pointed at herself and him—"wasn't a precursor to a post-game."

"Not that. Listen!"

They fell silent, and then she heard it. The gravel in the driveway popped and crunched underneath car tires. Nando's parents were home.

"Whoops. Guess that tongue will be sucking off priests sooner rather than later."

"Wait! Don't go out the front."

"Excuse me?"

Nando jumped up, anxiety overriding any shame or embarrassment he felt about his nakedness. He grabbed her arm and steered her away from the door. He was gentle about it, so she didn't break his nose. Not yet, anyway.

"What, you want me to slip out the servant's entrance?"

"Not exactly." He led her toward the window. Through it, she could see the headlights snap off. The crushed gravel glowed in the dim moonlight.

"Oh, no. No way."

"*Please*," he pleaded. "They'll kill me if they find out." Nando's grip tightened on her arm. "I'll give you four hundred dollars."

"What? Fuck you! I'm not a whore."

"Not for the sex. For climbing out the window. It's easy. I do it all the time."

She glanced out the window again, judging the difficulty. "Five hundred."

"Fine."

"And I get to drive your car for a month."

"A week."

"Two weeks."

"Okay, fine. Just go. *Please*." Nando slid open the large window. The chill air hit her and did Nando's naked form little favor. "Go that way. There's a wall around the corner that'll get you to the ground."

The thin vinyl rails of the window frame cut into her palms and her ass. *I should have asked for more.* She picked her way slowly across the darkened roof.

He called out to her, his voice quiet but pitched to carry. "I'll call you an Uber at the intersection."

Fuck. She forgot Nando had picked her up. The window slid shut before she could change her mind, and the curtains dropped, effectively blocking her from view. She hoped he was smart enough to light some incense to cover up the stench of sweat and sex. Otherwise, this was all for nothing.

Nando plodded from the window, completely enervated as the adrenaline drained away. Something on the floor caught his foot, and he stumbled a few steps, catching himself on the bed. With the curtains closed, what little light the sliver of moon shed was now cut off, and he couldn't see anything.

Probably the laptop charger. As soon as they made induction chargers for laptops, he was totally upgrading. Until then, he would ask his mom to call an electrician. This old house just didn't have enough plugs.

Flopping onto the bed, he buried his face into a pillow. As close a call as this was, even almost getting caught by his parents wasn't enough to dampen his mood.

I fucked Veronica Chambers.

Everyone knew she got around, but it wasn't like she was a total slut. She didn't fuck just anyone. With a deep breath, he could still smell her lingering scent on the sheets. He lay there, naked and with growing arousal as the memories flooded through him, his face buried in the pillow she had used.

His feet tangled in the sheets, but he paid it no mind. An hour ago, Veronica was pulling on those same sheets while he was tonsils-deep inside of her.

I can still taste her. He might never brush his teeth again.

The maid would have to change his sheets tomorrow. Silk felt good on the skin, and it impressed all the ladies—okay, the two of them who had graced his room—but they sure got clingy. His legs tangled in the grasping bedclothes, but he wasn't worried about that right now. Nando rolled onto his back, one hand pressing the pillow to his face so he could breathe in Veronica's lingering aroma. The other hand slid down his body and grasped his swollen cock.

He had made her scream. It wasn't like the pornos he watched. There wasn't an audience she was performing for. Just him. She *really* liked it when he used his mouth. His ears still rang with the sweet sound of her ecstasy.

His hand stroked, and he felt the familiar tingling in his toes and fingers as the orgasm built up. The tingling worked its way up his legs to his stomach. His chest tightened, and he had a fleeting thought that he was pressing the pillow too firmly to his face.

Is this what auto-erotic asphyxiation is like? If so, he understood the appeal. The sensation was intoxicating. His thoughts began to fog, blurring around the edges like the world's best high. It was almost painful but sharpened his focus. The pain drove back the orgasm, taking the euphoria to new heights.

It wasn't until he came, hot ejaculate splashing onto his doughy stomach, that he realized something was wrong. The waves of ecstasy were gone, a fleeting memory in his trembling muscles, but the pain lingered. The sensation wasn't just a tingle anymore. His skin burned like fire ants swarmed him. He ripped the pillow from his face and gasped a breath. The air didn't smell like Veronica anymore, but that gasp of air was sweet.

For a second, at least.

Until the pulsing, writhing tendrils dove into his mouth and burrowed down his throat.

"Honey?"

Carmen Alvarez knocked again. "Honey, did you fall asleep again? You know you aren't supposed to take naps. You'll just be up all night." The escitalopram did wonders to curb Ferdie's social anxiety, but the stuff did a real number on his circadian rhythm.

"Ferdie? Nando?" She remembered the nickname they were supposed to call him.

She knew she wasn't supposed to open the door without being invited—they'd had a family meeting about that where Ferdie had very passionately explained why he needed his privacy—but dinner had come and gone over an hour ago, and he wasn't responding to her texts—Ferdie's preferred method of speaking to his parents even when they were all home.

Carmen steeled herself and turned the knob. The door swung on oiled hinges without a single peep. She made a mental note to thank Jackson for that. It was important for the staff to hear when they were doing a good job.

A stench hit her that wrinkled her nose. A miasma of body odor, sweat, and something metallic.

He made us install a gym in the garage so that he could start exercising, and he insists on working out in his room. Teenage boys. Even after all these years, she was no closer to understanding them. Emmeline would have to shampoo Ferdie's room again. For the second time this year.

All the lights were off, even the TV—and that thing was hardly ever off—and the drapes were drawn. Carmen wasn't *that* old, but still, her eyes struggled to pierce the dark. Her hand swiped along the wall until she found the light switch.

When lights came on, she wished she hadn't been the one to check on their son.

THE ACCURSED

Nando lay in bed, naked, on his back. He was half sitting up like his body was propped on a pile of pillows. But it wasn't pillows that held him up.

Hundreds, thousands of thin dark roots pierced his body, lifting and anchoring him to the queen size bed beneath. His mouth and eyes gaped like he was terrified, but instead of horror, the cavities were filled with thick cords of wood, growing up, twining around other branches that grew from his chest and stomach. Slender branches sprouted from bright green nodes, and vestigial leaves the color of blood emerged from the buds at their tips.

15

When Sam got to Ash's house it looked like a Guns N' Roses' hotel room. Disemboweled throw pillows littered the floor, their guts scattered like freshly fallen snow. Their breakfast plates, which they'd left untouched as they rushed to the hospital, were no longer untouched. The plates lay on the floor, licked clean by Barkley.

Speaking of Barkley, the pup hurtled down the stairs and barrelled into Sam's legs. The small rescue wasn't yet a year old, but he was handful enough for an entire pack of dogs. After showering Sam with slobbery affection, Barkley careened through the kitchen and began to whine at the back door. He wasn't used to going so long without being let out, and a small stain on the kitchen rug was testament to that. Sam unlocked the sliding glass door leading to the backyard, and Barkley rushed through it, disappearing into the thicket that ringed the Williams' yard.

Sam's gaze took in the scene. The last thing he wanted was for Ash to come home to a destroyed house. She'd have her hands full with Mr. Williams' recuperation. He started in the kitchen because the house still smelled like eggs. The stink of old eggs churned his stomach. An hour later, Sam trudged out the front door, a bag of trash in one hand

and a bag of puppy supplies in the other. The trash went into the black container against the side fence, and the supplies went into the Tercel.

"Sammy! You didn't forget about me, did you, hon?"

Crap. He had completely forgotten about cleaning the Murrays' pool. Mrs. Murray peered at him through the blinds of her living room window.

"Um, no, Mrs. Murray. I was just fixing to come over. Gimme a minute, alright?" The blinds snapped closed, but not before she gave him a big smile.

He got into the Williams' house and leaned against the front door, banging his head against the metal-clad portal.

"Fuck." The last thing he wanted to do right then was service Mrs. Murray—he shook his head to get *that* thought out of his head.

Damnit, Ash. Why'd you have to start calling it that? Then again, there was nothing else he could do right then. He should be with Ash, but she definitely didn't want to see him right then. Maybe what he needed was a distraction.

Plus, me and mom could use the money. He made good money cleaning pools. Enough that it took a lot of strain off his mom, which was why he argued so much when she told him to concentrate on school for his senior year. Alice Dyer knew her son was working himself ragged to help out, but she also knew that he had plans after high school, plans that would be ruined if he let work get in the way. So, Sam relented and agreed to drastically reduce his workload.

The Tercel wasn't spacious by any means, but with some forethought, Sam could usually fit everything he needed in it. With the help of some bungee cords, he was even able to transport the pole he used for the pool brush and skimmer.

THE ACCURSED

Unfortunately, with everything going on with Judy and Mr. Williams, he'd completely forgotten about the job today, so he was going to have to make do. Luckily, the Williams had their own pool. Sam usually took care of the maintenance for them, and he knew Mr. W. wouldn't mind him using his tools.

Ten minutes later, Sam was back on the Murrays' front porch, a bucket full of supplies in one hand and a 16-foot telescopic pole resting on his right shoulder.

Mrs. Murray answered before he finished knocking. Her hair was pulled into a bun, aside from two long ringlets framing her face. She was barefoot, and her short silk robe barely reached down to her legs. The royal blue fabric would have billowed in the breeze if it weren't tied so tightly around her body. She, of course, had an afternoon cocktail clutched in one hand, the tropical-looking drink sweating with condensation.

God, I hope she's wearing something under that.

"I thought you forgot about me."

"I could never, Mrs. Murray." He was going for sincere but wasn't sure he quite made it.

She laughed like he'd made a joke. "You're too sweet. Mr. Murray doesn't want anyone going through the garage while his new toy is disassembled, so come on through the house. Wipe your sandals, please. We just got new carpets." She gestured with the bright blue slushie and turned, padding through the open-concept interior toward the back. "I see you remembered to dress for the weather."

Because I didn't want to get drenched in sweet tea again, you psycho. Sam hemmed and hawed over changing before he came over, but two things made him don the tank top, swim trunks, and flip flops he kept at Ash's house. He didn't want to deal with Mrs. Murray's shenanigans, and he didn't want to ruin the new outfit Ash bought him. Maintaining pools called for some caustic chemicals, after all.

"Yep. It's gonna be a warm one today."

"It sure is, Sammy."

Oh, lord, here it goes.

The glass door leading to the back deck was huge, about twenty feet long, and hinged to open like a massive accordion. It was already open, the lazy, warm spring air drifted through the house. The Murrays' backyard had a tropical theme. Tiki torches, patches of sand, bamboo decks. There were even palm trees. Not the tall palm trees you saw in movies. Winters in Elsbury were too cold for those. These were needle palms. They looked like someone decapitated a palm tree and left the head laying in the sand. More of a palm shrub than anything.

Aside from a fresh coat of stain on the decks, nothing had changed since he'd been here in the autumn. Sam unloaded his tools and supplies and got to it. He'd been doing this kind of work for a few years, so by this point he had everything down pat. Uncover the pool, clear the filters for the first time, skim the debris off the top, and then start the long process of brushing down the sides of the pool so the filter could clean the fine particulates out of the water.

By the time he finished brushing and sweeping, Sam was glad he'd opted to wear shorts and the tank top. The shirt was saturated with sweat, causing it to stick to his torso.

"Are you thirsty?"

Sam finished collapsing the pole and sat it down before turning to accept the lemonade Mrs. Murray always made him. "Definitely. Thanks, Mrs. Mur—" He saw what she was wearing—or rather, not wearing. Gone was the blue silk robe. In its place was a bright yellow bikini...if it could be called that. The thing she wore was all straps like she'd been cocooned by a spider with a flair for the dramatic. It covered all the necessary bits. But just barely.

Sam didn't know if it was cosmetics or if she'd won the genetic jackpot, but despite being a mother in her 40s or maybe late 30s—he was terrible with ages—Mrs. Murray had kept things tight. Realizing his mouth was hanging open, he shut it with an audible click.

Mrs. Murray smiled, her eyes inscrutable behind large sunglasses. She held out a large glass of lemonade, a cube of pineapple speared on the rim. It was sweet and tangy, just how Sam liked it, and he wondered if she intended for her bikini to match the drink. Tipping it back gave him an excuse to rip his eyes away from all the exposed, and he gulped until the drink was gone.

"Can I jump in yet?"

The ice clacked in the empty glass, and Sam gasped a breath after the long drought. Instead of meeting her gaze, he turned toward the pool. "I still have to check the heater and figure out what's going on with the pump."

"Is something the matter?"

"Do you hear that?" They fell quiet until the only sounds were the breeze, the gentle rumble of distant cars, and the angry hum of the pool pump. As they listened, the whine of the motor changed pitch, pulsing as it struggled to draw in water. He looked to her, keeping his eyes up. "I think the main drain is clogged."

Sam figured as much from the beginning, but he hoped brushing the grate at the bottom of the pool would clear whatever blockage there was. Unfortunately, it hadn't. He would have to go down and see what was going on for himself.

The smallest of frowns crinkled Mrs. Murray's face, and she pouted. "I was hoping to get wet soon."

Sam ignored the double entendre. "It'll just be a minute to fix."

16

This wasn't the first time Sam had to clean out someone's main drain.

God, I'm starting to talk like her. I need to get out of here.

The work was gross but fast. Clearing out a clogged drain was his least favorite part of the job. It was fair to say that watching him strip and jump into the water probably made it Mrs. Murray's favorite. He did his best to ignore her piercing gaze and how it tracked his every move. Sam loved working on rich people's pools. The heated water wasn't as much of a shock to jump into. Not that there were many pool owners in Elsbury who weren't rich. The water was warm, but not so warm that it wasn't refreshing against his overheated skin.

After clearing the drain, all Sam had to do was check the heat pump. Luckily, what little mechanical knowledge Sam had was limited to pool heating and filtration systems. If the Tercel ever broke down—actually, it was more a matter of *when*, not *if*—he was screwed, but he could keep pool systems running. Sam had completed the annual maintenance on the Murrays' heat pump last time he was there, so this time was really just a cursory inspection.

Within a few minutes of finishing, Sam had collected his gear and was standing at the Murrays' back door, dripping onto the patio. "I'm all done, Mrs. Murray. I forgot to bring a towel, and I don't want to track water everywhere." There was no response from the house.

"Sam."

He jumped and twisted, only just remembering the collapsed eight-foot pole he carried and stopping it before he brained Mrs. Murray with it. "Jesus! You startled me."

She smiled, and for the first time, he realized her cheeks dimpled. Sam was already taller than her, and being on the top step of the deck, he towered over her. The strappy bikini left a wide expanse of cleavage exposed, impossible to ignore when looking down at her.

"Can you get me a towel, please? I don't want to track water into the house."

"Sorry, no can do. No one's allowed on the new carpet covered in pool water. You'll have to shower off first."

Sam wished he'd put his tank top back on. "Oh, um...That's okay. I'll just go through the garage."

She sidestepped and cut him off, shaking her head. "Mr. Murray's new hotrod is in there, and he hates it when anyone else goes in." She rolled her eyes. "Men and their cars. Sorry, Sammy. But you'll have to use the outdoor shower."

Sam considered making a run for it. He was probably faster than her, even laden down with a bucket of tools and the pole. *Fuck, she hasn't paid me yet.* That settled it, he had to play her game for a while longer.

Mrs. Murray turned and led him back toward the pool. Against the house on the other side of the small outdoor kitchen, the Murrays had a small bathroom. It was tiled in dark greens and blues, so the confined space felt like you were drowning in the ocean. Unfortunately, it was only a half-bath with a toilet and small sink. The shower was just outside the bathroom. It was plumbed so water would come straight down from the dark bronze head and tiled in natural stone. If it weren't for the five-foot-high bamboo panel, anyone using it would be completely exposed to the backyard.

Sam managed to hold back a scowl but only barely. "Do you have any towels? I'll rinse off really quick."

Mrs. Murray went into the bathroom and emerged with a thick white towel, draping it on a black wire rack. "Best use the soap. Oh, and make sure you give those a good ring out. We don't want any chlorine getting on the new carpet."

He dropped the tools and gave Mrs. Murray a tight-lipped smile. "Of course." Kicking off his flip flops, he cranked the knobs to get the water running. Water gushed out of the showerhead like it was raining. A wide, heavy stream of water splashed down. If he weren't so upset, he may have enjoyed the experience. The Murrays' outdoor shower was nicer than his indoor shower.

As it was, Sam wasn't very happy. Before he dared take off his swim trunks, he waited until Mrs. Murray was sitting in one of the lounge chairs beside the pool. He scooted the bamboo partition until he was satisfied she couldn't see anything through the crack where the panels hinged together. With a grunt, Sam yanked the clingy trunks off and started rinsing them. He went so far as to get a good lather of soap going and actually wash the garment. The last thing he wanted was Mrs. Murray trying to get him into her son's shorts again because his had traces of chlorine. The trunks were synthetic, and water wrung out of them easily. Tossing them over the towel rack, Sam stepped fully into the shower.

The deluge hit him like a wall of water. It had excellent pressure, and after over an hour of brushing the swimming pool, it felt glorious on his aching muscles. It had been a warm day, but the breeze had wicked away the sweat and water and whatever heat his body had accumulated. The goosebumps on his body disappeared. It was like climbing into a warm bed after a long day.

Keeping with the tropical theme, the shampoo smelled of coconut. There wasn't any facewash, so, guy that he was, the shampoo did double duty. His face turned to the sky, and he let the water rinse away the suds. His tense muscles weren't just due to the work. Everything that had happened with Mr. Williams, with Judy...with him and Ash...not to mention the ever-present stress of having to have perfect grades, worrying about his mom working too much, and wanting to help her however he could.

It all weighed on him, and he exhaled a deep breath, trying to let the worries swirl down the drain with the water and carpet-ruining chemicals. Even if it was just for a few minutes. The water pounded on his shoulders, driving out the ache of more than just tense muscles. He picked up the bar of soap and closed his eyes to better enjoy the heat on his face, lathering up his chest and stomach.

"Need help getting your back?"

His eyes flew open, and he fought the urge to turn around. The natural stone was rough and lumpy as he pressed himself against it. The soap slipped out of his hands and plopped in the shallow puddle at his feet.

THE ACCURSED

"What—what are you doing? I'm naked!" He cranked his head to look over his shoulder. Mrs. Murray was bent over picking up the soap. When she stood, his eyes bulged. The strappy bikini was gone, and so were her sunglasses, but those were less relevant to the situation at hand.

"I noticed." Stepping forward, Mrs. Murray passed through the downstream of water, moving her head aside so her hair didn't get wet. The water crashed into her shoulders and breasts, dimpling her supple flesh. Streams of the clear liquid sluiced off her breasts, funneling down her cleavage in a thick torrent. Smaller rivulets of water trickled from her nipples, the darker skin pursed like they were waiting for a kiss. With another step, she exited the water. Beads of it clung to her like sparkling dewdrops. She rubbed her palms together, working up a thick lather of white bubbles, and then before he could say anything, her hands were on his shoulders, kneading his muscles and spreading the suds over his back.

"Um—um—um—I don't think this was built for two. If you don't mind waiting, I'll be done in a minute." Closing his eyes, he tried to ignore the sensation of her cool, smooth palms running up and down his back.

"You poor, sweet boy. Pining after that girl when she doesn't even see you."

"Um...what?" His thoughts whirled like the vortex of water funneling down the drain at their feet. "No—no, it—it's fine. Veronica and I are probably going to the dance together."

She leaned closer. He could feel the heat of her body radiating into his, could feel the supple flesh of her breasts pressing against his back.

"She flounces around with that spoiled rugby player right in front of you. Rubbing your face in it."

Oh. She means Ash. Pressing against the stone wall, he shook his head as best he could. "No, it's not like that. We're just friends—best friends since we were kids."

"She settles for sirloin when she could have Wagyu tenderloin." Her hands kneaded and lathered farther down his back.

"I...I don't know what that means, but thanks, I guess. Um, I think I can handle it from here. Thanks for—woah!" Mrs. Murray's hands slid from his lower back down to his ass. Without thinking, Sam twirled around, jerking his tender buns out of her clutches and almost slipping on the soapy floor.

Mrs. Murray's eyes flew open, and her jaw dropped. Too late, Sam realized what he'd done. He may have taken his buns out of the frying pan, but he'd put something much more delicate right in the fire.

"Oh, Sammy... I knew you had a gift, but I never suspected..." Her eyes were locked on like a hawk diving for its dinner.

He wanted to yell *Hey, eyes up here!* "Um..." was all he could think to say.

Her gaze snapped to his, and she stepped forward, leaning until her mouth was a hair's breadth from his ear, her breasts pressing against his chest. He tried to back away, but the stone wall was immovable. He settled for wishing with all his heart that Mr. Murray didn't choose that moment to come home.

"She doesn't deserve you, Sammy."

It took him a moment to remember what she had been talking about.

THE ACCURSED

"She doesn't see you. Doesn't see how you treat her, how you care for her." Her hands pressed against his abdomen. He flinched as they brushed his sides—despite the circumstances, he was still very much ticklish. Her voice was a throaty whisper. "She doesn't deserve you." Her left hand drifted down his stomach, past his waist, and she grabbed a handful of him. They both uttered a low moan, for similar, but very different reasons.

Mrs. Murray reached up and adjusted the showerhead so the cascading stream gushed over them. The liquid pooled between their chests, dribbling down their sides in thick rivulets. A stream ran down her left arm, curled around the back of her hand, and trickled down his balls. Despite himself, a throb slammed through his body. Mrs. Murray smirked, then slowly began to pump her hand, a faint scent of coconuts wafting with each stroke.

"I think..." The words caught in his throat. "I think it's clean now..."

"Shhh, Sammy. I'll give you everything you deserve. I've wanted this for *so long*."

His eyes fluttered closed. "What about—" He had to swallow before the words would come. "What about Mr. Murray?"

"I don't begrudge him his fun, and he doesn't begrudge me mine."

What would it hurt? He didn't know where the thought came from, but it was hard to argue with. It was hard to concentrate, to think of a reason why he should stop Mrs. Murray. His eyes fluttered and another moan slipped through his lips.

What about Veronica? What about Ash? The thoughts slammed through his brain, with them came his mental faculties. If he weren't pressed against the hard rock wall he'd have jerked away from Mrs.

Murray's warm body. He opened his mouth to stop her, but before the first syllable could form, a new voice rang out.

"Mom! What the hell?" Mike Murray's eyes were wide, confusion and fury on his face. "*Sam?* Dude, what the actual fuck? You're bangin' my mom?"

Sam pushed away from the wall and wrenched—ahem, *himself*—out of Mrs. Murray's grasp. "No, Mike, it's not like—"

"Holy shit, dude! Do you have a concealed carry permit for that canon?" Mike took an involuntary step back, tripping over the towel rack and going down.

"Honey!" Mrs. Murray slipped in the soapy water and almost went down, too, but she skidded her way to her son, reaching to help him up. Mike vacillated between accepting her help and not wanting to be near his naked mom or grabbing *that* hand.

What the fuck am I doing here? The towel and his clothes were draped over the towel rack, underneath the struggling teenager. Sam didn't want to go anywhere near Mrs. Murray's reach.

He ran. The Murrays would just have to deal with water, soap, and chlorine getting on their new carpet. Sam didn't slow down as he barreled out the front door, down the porch, across the yard, and over the hedge. It was still broad daylight, but his pale ass ran like it was on fire. A car's horn blared, but Sam didn't look back to see if it had anything to do with him. It was his first experience running naked, especially with a full-on erection. He did *not* recommend it.

Slamming the door behind him, he threw the bolt and slumped against it. Hands on knees, he bent double to catch his breath. All his tools, supplies, and clothes were still next door, but there was no way he was going back for them. And he definitely wasn't going to be asking Mrs. Murray for his pay. He would have to come up with a reason for the Williams to move. There was no way he could face Mrs. Murray again.

Or Mike. Oh, god... What would Sam do when he saw Mike at school? It was a good thing it was Spring Break. Maybe everything would blow over by the time they returned to school.

Another honk sounded from the street, and Sam cringed. Then he realized that the Williams' front door had a full glass panel. It was decorative glass, but with his bare ass pressed against it, there was no denying that he was mooning the entire neighborhood.

"Fuck me!" He threw himself away from the door and ran to Ash's room where his outfit from earlier was waiting.

17

Fully dressed again, Sam slid open the back door and called for Barkley. A pang of guilt stabbed through his gut. He'd completely forgotten about the pup when he went over to clean the pool. Luckily, the furball had a lot of pent-up energy after being cooped up all day, and he was used to being left outside for long stretches of time.

He called again, but there was no corresponding bark or yip, not even the rustling of grass. The Williams' property stretched far beyond the established, well-maintained backyard. Beyond the pool and short-cut grass, the property faded into untamed wilderness. Young Ash and Sam spent many hours exploring it. Sam didn't know how far exactly, but it stretched back far enough for a couple young kids to consider it unchartered territory.

With a furtive glance toward the neighbor's—the Williams' backyard was in clear view of Mr. and Mrs. Murrays' bedroom windows—Sam stepped into the backyard and walked to the edge of where it turned from yard to overgrown wilderness.

"Barkley! Here, boy!" Still nothing. Sam grimaced, stepping into the tall grass. *I better not get a tick on me.*

Picking a path that he hadn't trodden in years, Sam wound his way through the tall grass and sparse trees until he came to a clearing.

"Barkley!"

Still no barking, but a rustling came from a small copse of oaks. The tree trees were clumped together, stymying each other's growth. The breeze played tricks on Sam's eyes and made it look like the low grass around the trunks were squiggling.

Grass, twigs, dead leaves, and pine needles crunched underfoot. It was spring, but the aroma of dead things was still prevalent in the air. The pungent, earthy scene of decomposing leaves, mostly.

"Barkley?" More rustling, and now that he was closer, Sam was certain it wasn't just the wind blowing through the brush. The bark was rough, and it bit into his palms as he leaned between two trees to peer to the other side.

The rustling sound grew louder, and Sam turned his head toward it. The steady breeze cut off suddenly, and the sound died with it. Before Sam could call for the dog again, he heard a steady *thump-thump-thump*. Whatever it was, it was getting closer.

Suddenly, a brown ball of fur and slobber leapt through the underbrush, his overlarge paws beating a basso beat against the thick duff on the ground.

Barkley jumped into Sam's chest and proceeded to share his slobber.

"Hey, Bark—yech! Ew, no kisses, Barkley!" It took a few minutes to calm the dog down, but soon they headed back to the house. "C'mon, boy. You're going to stay with me for a while."

Barkley may have been a young dog, but he knew a car ride when he saw one, and his tail wagged like he was a helicopter readying for liftoff.

THE ACCURSED

Sam practically ran out of the house and to his car, praying to whatever gods or deities were watching that there wouldn't be an angry mob or husband waiting for him.

The drive to Sam's house was too short for Barkley's liking. He whined as Sam slowed to a stop, but if the layers of slobber dripping down the passenger side door were any indication, he still enjoyed it, no matter how brief.

His mom's car was in the driveway. He half expected her to be down at the hospital visiting Mr. Williams, but she was probably giving Ash space and time to be with her father alone.

"Hey, Mom," he called when he and Barkley entered. "Barkley is gonna stay with us until they figure out what's going on with Mr. Williams." He unhooked the leash, and Barkley was off like a cannonball, barking and sniffing the ground like he was tracking something. Sam deposited his keys and wallet on the shelf by the door and followed the eager pup. No doubt he'd want to head into the backyard and start exploring.

"Did you already have dinner? I'm starv—"

His voice cut off when he saw his mom lying on the floor. Rushing to her side, he dropped to his knees.

"Mom!"

Her checkbook and pen lay beside her like she was balancing her account when she fell. He put his fingers to her throat, but he was too shaken up to feel the pulse.

"Mom!"

18

"How are you doing?" Ash ran her hand along the back of Sam's head and squeezed his shoulder.

"As good as you are right now, I expect."

The hospital waiting room had to be one of the loneliest and saddest places in the entire facility. Worried people gathered there to await news, hoping with all their hearts for the best, but knowing deep down that their world was about to change forever. Two other people sat in the waiting room, a middle-aged man and a girl no more than ten or eleven at his side. They wore matching expressions of worry, though the girl busied herself with toys that had been in the waiting room longer than Sam had been alive. The man watched her with a sad, unknowable expression on his face.

Sixteen hours ago, the ambulance brought Alice Dyer to the hospital. Sixteen hours Sam had been waiting for answers. Ash had been waiting even longer.

"Thank you for taking care of Barkley." She bumped his shoulder with her own.

The ambulance's sirens had brought out the neighbors. Trailing the stretcher that carried his mom, Sam had maintained enough sense to ask the neighbor girl, Janiece, to watch over Barkley.

"What the fuck is happening—" He cut off when someone sat down in the chair across the aisle from them.

"Oh, hello there," the old woman said. It took Sam more than a few moments to recognize the little old lady from the thrift shop. Luckily, Ash remembered her name.

"Hey, Dottie."

"It's nice of you to come visit Judy. She'd appreciate it."

Ash tensed beside him, no doubt feeling guilty for not visiting her old friend. He couldn't blame her, though, not after everything that had happened with her dad. Sam hadn't spared Judy a single thought until this moment.

"Actually, we're here visiting my dad and his mom."

"Oh, you poor dears. I'm so sorry. Is everything alright?"

"They're unconscious."

Dottie's back was as bent as a question mark, but right then, it straightened. "In comas? Same as Judy?"

"No." Sam's voice was more forceful than he intended. In truth, he didn't know what was going on with his mom. They were still waiting for test results, but he didn't want her to be in a coma.

"Dear, dear. What is going on in this town?"

Sam stiffened at the question. That's exactly what he was going to ask Ash when Dottie walked in.

"Maybe there's a gas leak in town," Ash suggested. "Like in the shop."

THE ACCURSED

Dottie shook her head, her little feet kicking as she scooted forward in her chair. "This is just like what happened in Dunwich."

"What happened in Dunwich?" Ash and Sam asked at the same time.

"Don't you remember that couple I was telling you about the other day?"

Sam looked to Ash, at a loss for words. He didn't remember speaking to Dottie at all. Ash's brows furrowed. When she spoke, the words came slowly. "The couple who died."

Dottie's mane of white hair bobbed. "Yes! A couple of poofs in Dunwich died just a few weeks ago."

"Poofs?"

Dottie waved a hand that looked more like a withered chicken foot. "Gays. Homosexuals. I can't keep up with what they're calling themselves now."

This was going in the direction of one of those "Okay, Boomer" conversations that Sam would rather not be around for. Dottie didn't seem to notice their discomfort and continued.

"There was a couple of old poofs in Dunwich, not much younger than I. They didn't get out much, but when the mail started to pile, the city went in and found them. One of them dead in bed. The other had fallen down the stairs. Both dry as raisins like they'd been there years instead of days. Still no idea what caused it other than they had some weird skin condition."

Sam couldn't help but lean closer. "So, what, you think that whatever killed those guys is killing people here in Elsbury?"

"If not that then what?"

"But Dad, Alice, and Judy aren't dead. They're in a coma."

Dottie nodded like Ash had just proven her point. "The poofs in Dunwich had been in comas. When they did the autopsy, they found that both were malnourished and dehydrated."

Ash wasn't convinced. "You said one of them fell down the stairs."

"Maybe he woke up disoriented and fallen."

"But that—"

Dottie threw up her hands. "I wasn't there, was I? I'm just telling you what I heard on the news."

Ash's lips pursed like she wanted to disagree further. "But the police said it was a gas leak that put Judy in a coma."

Dottie laughed and had to clutch her mouth to keep her dentures in. "Gas leak? The pilot light at the store hasn't been lit in two weeks. Judy's been so busy she hasn't fixed it yet."

"Then why did they say it was?"

"Men. They can't stand not knowing. Especially doctors. The more education, the more they don't like not knowing." She glanced at Sam apologetically.

But Sam wasn't listening. "Can you excuse us for a second?" He grabbed Ash's arm and stood, dragging her out of the waiting room.

"Where are we going?"

Sam ignored her and led them down the hallway, reading the signs on the walls. Finally, he pulled her into an empty room.

"What are we doing in the chapel? Don't tell me you found god?"

"We're not here to pray." He walked her to the front pew and tugged her into sitting beside him. "We need to talk."

"We could've talked in the waiting room."

He shook his head. "Did you hear what Dottie said?"

"Don't tell me you think there's some sort of virus going around putting people in comas. You think a pandemic is causing this?"

"I don't think it's as simple as a virus."

"What do you think it is then?"

"I think it's the curse."

Incredulity laced her voice, and she cackled. "You really think that some painting from the 1800s is causing people to go into comas?"

"How would you explain it then?" Sam jumped up from the pew and started pacing. "How else can you explain so many people having accidents and going into comas? What are the chances?"

"And you think it's more likely that some magical painting is to blame? That's more likely than, I don't know, some scientific explanation?"

"Can *you* come up with a scientific explanation?"

"No, but that doesn't prove anything. And it certainly doesn't prove that there's a supernatural cause for all this."

"What are the chances that my mom, your dad, and Judy all fall into comas within a day of each other?"

Ash was silent for a moment. "I don't know. *Really* unlikely? But still, Sam—"

"I know!" he said, frustration lacing his tone. He scrubbed his eyes with his palms, growling in frustration. When he looked at her, he could barely contain his fear. "But...what if it's true?"

Ash couldn't meet his gaze, and her eyes lingered on the various religious symbols around the room. A Star of David. A cross with Jesus on it. She picked at her cuticles—something she only did when she was anxious or worrying. Finally, she looked at him.

"I'm not saying it is real…" Sam stayed quiet, nodding along. "But, and this is a big but—and don't you dare make the obvious joke—*if* it is real, then I guess it's better to be safe than sorry."

"Meaning what?"

"Meaning I'd rather take the chance of looking like a fool and be right than do nothing and be wrong. With that said, what do we do?"

He dropped into the pew beside her. "The painting said that the couple needs to…to cleave before the full moon."

"The *new* moon," she corrected. "What? I remember it being a new moon specifically because… Well, you know."

"The books." Sam's voice was flat.

"You're not gonna give me crap about that *now,* are you?"

Sam sighed. "You're right. Not the time to get into your terrible taste in vampire fiction." Ash issued a low growl, but he continued. "Okay, so the couple must cleave before the new moon. How long does that give us?"

Ash already had her cell phone out. The screen lit up as her fingers swiped across the screen. Within moments, she had the answer. "The new moon is this Thursday."

"Four days. That's enough time, right?"

"Enough time for what, exactly?"

"To cleave."

"And by 'cleave,' we're assuming…" Her voice trailed off, waiting for him to pick it up.

Sam sucked in a quick breath. "To…have sex?" He turned toward the large wooden crucifix to hide his blush. Thoughts whirled through his mind. If the curse or blessing or whatever was real, and he and Ash unleashed it, did that mean that *they* were the couple?

Does that mean...

Ash leaned forward to look at him, but he pretended like he was studying the crucifix. "You know what this means?"

His stomach turned to cold jelly. Did she just realize what they needed to do? "What?" He wouldn't be the first person to say it.

"You're going to have to fuck Veronica."

"What!?" Sam leapt to his feet again, nearly tripping on the pew's leg. That *definitely* wasn't what he had been thinking.

"Randy's out of town. You've been pining after Veronica since freshman year. You're gonna have to lay the pipe like your mother's life depends on it." Despite the circumstances, mirth danced in Ash's eyes. "Because it does."

Sam slumped into the pew like he'd melted. He wasn't sure if he was excited, relieved, disappointed, or terrified. He couldn't lie, getting with Veronica *had* been the most played out scenario in his spank bank for years. On the other hand, he had all these new thoughts and...feelings for Ash. And then there was the fact that this all started with the two of them. *True love's kiss to begin...*that was what the painting said, and that was when things started going bad. Since they were the ones who kissed, did that mean they had to be the ones to have sex?

The thought sent equal amounts of terror, anxiety, and elation through him. He was still unsure about his feelings for her. He wasn't sure if he'd gotten over her years ago, if he had a crush on her, or if he was just confused and had the world's biggest pair of blue balls.

But she was right. Sam had been pining after Veronica for a long time. And he definitely wouldn't be the one to suggest that he and

Ash had to end the curse themselves. She had a boyfriend...and she'd never shown the slightest bit of interest toward him.

She's right, and Veronica is the safest bet. Actually...*Speaking of safe bets...* He dropped his head into his hands and groaned.

"Don't be such a baby. It won't be that bad."

"That's not it." His voice was muffled under his hands until he scrubbed at his face and looked at her. "We're operating under the assumption that we just need to have sex to end this thing, right?" Her eyes flashed and he hurried to add, "That *one of us* needs to have sex, right?"

She looked at him through squinted eyes before finally nodding. "If you're thinking about hiring a working girl, I don't think we have any of those in Elsbury."

"I'm not talking about hiring a whore!" A gasp had them turning their heads to the entrance of the chapel. An older woman with one hand on a metal cane and the other on an IV stand stood there, glaring at them with righteous indignation.

"Wait, that's not what it sounded like..." But the old lady already turned and tottered off.

Ash was doubled over in her seat, laughing. Sam scooted next to her and dropped his voice.

"I'm talking about Mrs. Murray."

"I don't think she has sex for money, Sam."

"Aargh! No, listen. Something happened earlier..." Sam spent the next five minutes telling Ash what happened at the Murrays', and then the next ten minutes convincing her he was telling the truth. When she finally relented and said she believed him, they lapsed into silence.

THE ACCURSED

He didn't know why, but waiting for her to say something was just as bad as waiting for the doctors to give him news about his mom.

"So, you're telling me that he actually said that? About the concealed carry permit?"

Sam's mouth dropped open. "That's what you've taken out of all this?" He had originally omitted a few details. Mrs. Murray giving him half a hand job and Mike's exclamation, to be specific, but Ash had known he was holding something back, and she badgered him until he relented and spilled all the sordid details.

"Credit where credit's due. It's not just anyone who could come up with a quip like that when they've just seen their mom getting railed."

Sam spluttered. "I was not—! We were not—!"

Ash laughed so hard tears streamed down her face. "Oh, man. Your face! I wish I had a picture of it. No! Actually, I wish I had a picture of your bare, soapy ass booking it out of there."

"Ash!" Sam slumped into the pew and prayed for death.

Her howls of laughter plagued the room for minutes. Finally, the gales of mirth receded into chuckles.

"Are you done?"

Ash wiped tears from her cheeks, her face flushed. "I guess—I guess you could say…that the hedge wasn't the only bush in the front yard today!"

"Gods, give me strength."

The chapel echoed with Ash's laughter once again.

"Okay. Okay, I'm done." Small chuckles interrupted every other word. "Sorry, I'm done for now."

"For now?"

"Oh yeah. Don't think for one second you're going to live this down any time soon."

Sam groaned in despair but sat up. "Okay…about Mrs. Murray—" Sam shot Ash a sharp glare, but her face twitched only once. "She seems like a sure thing. She's probably the safest bet, right?"

"You sound like you just want an excuse to fuck Mrs. Murray."

"I do not!"

"I'm just saying…" Ash held up her hands, a grin stretching one side of her mouth.

"If I wanted to fuck her, she'd be well and truly fucked."

"Jeesh, someone's a little cocky." The grin took to both sides of her mouth this time.

"That's not what I meant, and you know it." He crossed his arms and tried not to sulk. "She'd been all but throwing herself at me for years now. All I'm saying is that if I really wanted to, it would have happened already."

"You got pretty close today."

Memories flooded Sam's mind. Mrs. Murray's bikini, the water gushing down her naked body, the heat of her breasts pressed against him. He shifted uncomfortably in the pew and cleared his throat. "Today was different. Before she was content to leave it at veiled come-ons and suggestive outfits. She was… It was like something came over her."

"I think she was looking for some**one** to come over her."

"Haha."

"Setting aside the cougar's motivations, it would be a solid plan."

"Would be?"

Ash nodded. "Yep. Unfortunately, the Murrays are going to Aspen for Spring Break. They asked me to keep an eye on the place."

"That was before their son caught his mom with my dick in her hand."

"Thanks for painting *that* lovely image"—Sam blushed and turned away—"but I think Mrs. Murray's proclivities were news only to little Mikey. She's been my neighbor for ten years. Trust me, yours isn't the first dick she's held out of wedlock."

"Dear lord, Ash..."

"You started it."

Sam waved it away, wanting more than anything to move past this horrifying conversation. "Okay, so where does that leave us?"

Ash jumped to her feet and brushed imaginary dust off like she was readying for work. "That means it's time to sack up, put on your big boy panties, and go fuck Veronica to end this curse."

"Jesus. You really know how to suck the fun out of things." Sam shook his head, exasperated. With much less verve than she showed, he got to his feet. "Besides, how am I supposed to go from the guy who's barely said a word to her for six years to getting in her pants? We only have four days."

"Don't sweat it. I'll take care of it. I've got a plan."

"Why do you seem so eager for this? And what do you mean you'll take care of it?"

Her smile stretched ear to ear. "This is exciting!" Her squeal reverberated a hundred times throughout the chapel. "Even if the curse is bullshit—which it most likely is, and by that I mean it *definitely* is—this means that massive boner you've been lugging around for Veronica will finally get taken care of." Before Sam could protest about how that was the wrong thing to focus on right now, she continued. "Also, Veronica has a...let's call it a *reputation*. It shouldn't be that hard to set you guys up."

"What, you're saying she's a whore?"

"'Whore' is a strong word. Let's just say she takes charge of her sexuality."

"That doesn't sound much better."

"We don't have time to dissect your antiquated misogynistic notions of proper female sexual behavior."

"I didn't mean—"

"No time! C'mon, let's go get you laid."

Sam didn't have the heart to argue his merits as a feminist. Ash rushed from the nondenominational chapel with a smile on her face and a pep in her step. If nothing else, it was the first time he'd seen her excited for something since she got the call about her dad.

Okay... Time to save the world and bang a girl.

19

Ugh. How did people survive before cell phones?

Ash had spent the last two hours cruising through Elsbury looking for Veronica. If she'd texted it would've taken a few minutes to find her, but she wanted running into Veronica to be organic. If she arranged to meet her, it would be weird for Ash to immediately start talking about Sam. It wasn't like she and Veronica were friends, so any amount of intentional contact would be suspect from the start.

I'm probably overthinking this. But it wasn't like she'd played matchmaker before. She was just winging it. Veronica did have a reputation, after all. Maybe a text was all she needed. Like a bow and arrow, maybe Ash just needed to aim her toward Sam's bullseye.

Then again, they needed every advantage if this thing was going to work...so, she did things the old-fashioned way. She hit all the hot spots, such as they were in Elsbury, looking for Sam's crush.

And it took *forever*.

Ash finally found herself at the mall. It was the last place to search other than Veronica's house, and she definitely wasn't going there without texting first.

It was Monday and still early, so there weren't many shoppers out. There were more kids than usual, but that was because it was Spring Break and there wasn't much else to do in Elsbury. The food court in the center of the mall was always the busiest, so Ash headed there and scanned the crowd.

Ash was, at the best of times, a single broken nail or one bitchy comment away from losing her shit, and playing detective was really pissing her off. Passing by the long-broken fountain in the center of the food court, Ash spotted Scott. It was rare to see him out of Randy's orbit, so it took a double-take to confirm it was really him. Pretending not to notice him, she quickened her pace, but her luck—shitty as it was—was consistent if nothing else.

"Hey, baby girl. What's up?"

Ash closed her eyes and counted to five before turning. He was wearing a matching royal blue ensemble, hat, shirt, jeans, and shoes.

"Hey, Scott. I thought you were leaving town for Spring Break."

Damn. That sounded too much like a question. The last thing she wanted was to encourage a conversation with the skeeve.

"Nah, I'm stuck here. Gotta work later. Wanna hang?" He smiled, and to his credit, the smile was only marginally creepy.

Still, she shook her head. If she gave him even the slightest bit of hope, she'd spend the rest of the day trying to ditch him. "Sorry, can't. I'm meeting Veronica for lunch. Have you seen her?"

"That fine-ass chica? Yeah, I seen her. Over at Marston's a little bit ago."

The disappointment must've been clear on her face. The Elsbury Mall wasn't that big, but Ash had been on her feet for hours, and Marston's was as far from the food court as it got.

THE ACCURSED

Scott gave her a wide smile as if reading her mind. "I got you. We can cut through the warehouse. Come on." He waved at her to follow.

Ash was so used to Scott being one of Randy's ever-present hangers-on that she had forgotten that he worked at the Pretzel Factory in the mall. The part of her that wanted to escape warred with the part that desperately wanted to be off her feet. Her feet won.

They wove their way through the crowded food court and through a set of double doors that did a decent job of blending in with the wall. On the other side was a narrow cinderblock hallway, lit by harsh fluorescent lights. It was a scene that belonged in a horror movie, sections of light dissected by globs of inky shadows.

"This way." Scott led her left, down the hallway. The sounds of their footsteps echoed in the concrete tube. It opened into a large, communal warehouse shared by all the merchants in that wing of the mall. Steel warehouse racking bordered the walls and dozens of pallets of merchandise lined the floor. Scott turned down a row of pallets, and she followed. Rubbing her arms, she shivered. It was cold. The mall probably didn't bother to warm the warehouse.

After about a minute of walking, the corridor of pallets widened into a small clearing, a half dozen camp chairs circled as if around a campfire. Three empty pallets with flattened cardboard boxes atop them lined one side of the clearing, like hobo beds.

"What is this place?"

Scott laughed and pulled a joint from his pocket, lighting it. "This is where we take our breaks. Managers don't know about it." He held out the lit joint to her and she shook her head. "Come on, it'll warm you up."

"No, thanks."

He patted his pocket. "Or I got something stronger if you want that'll really perk you up..."

Shaking her head again, she scanned the darkened hideaway, and another shiver ran through her. "This place is creepy. Which way to Marston's?"

Scott took a long hit, held it in, and exhaled all in a rush. "Don't worry." His voice came out in a squeak. "Come sit down with me." He patted the camp chair beside him.

She should have known better than to accept help from Scott. He was just using it as an excuse to check her out some more. This time without the danger of doing it where Randy could see. "Whatever." She turned around intending to head back.

Scott scrambled to his feet and cut her off. "What's the hurry, chica?"

"Don't call me that."

"Come on, don't be like that. You gotta be lonely with Randy out of town."

"Not really." She tried to step around him, but he was faster than he looked and blocked her again. *It's probably all that matching Adidas. Added horsepower or something.* "Get out of my way."

"Come oooon," he wheedled, pacing her so she couldn't get past him. "I know you gave it up. Gave Randy that warm Elsbury welcome, so it's not like you're saving it up for anything special." Judging by the sneer, he thought he was laying some smooth lines on her. "Have you ever fucked stoned? It's wild." The joint dangled from his mouth, bouncing with each word. She tried again to dodge around him, but he was there. Leaning in close, he dropped his voice to a whisper. "Randy don't gotta know."

His fetid breath sent shivers down her spine like oily spiders were crawling all over her. She blew a long breath through her nose, then smiled and looked at him through her eyelashes. When Scott saw it, his grin spread ear to ear.

"Alright…"

He leaned closer, and Ash couldn't stop her gorge from rising. With a quick jerk, Ash sent his balls rocketing into his torso with her knee.

Scott squealed in a sound that was neither smooth, sexy, nor manly. He collapsed like a felled tree, and this time, he didn't block her as she stepped around him.

"Don't worry, Scotty. It's not like you're saving it up for anything special." She debated kicking him again, but her feet already hurt, and she couldn't rule out the possibility that touching him would transmit some sort of disease.

She did it anyway.

The warehouse was dimly lit, but their path was easy enough to backtrack. She didn't know why, but tears streamed down her face as she fast-walked through the warehouse. Scott had always been a creep, but she thought he was a harmless creep. As soon as she got out of there, she was going to call Randy.

A shattered testicle will be the least of his problems then.

The door groaned in protest as she slammed into it, and she stumbled out of the hallway into the food court. She glanced back before it closed to make sure Scott wasn't behind her. Not sure why, maybe she'd watched too many horror movies. Not watching where she was going, she collided with someone, her elbow smashing into their ribs.

"Oof! Miss Williams? Is something the matter?" Strong arms stopped her from falling.

Ash jerked her head and saw Mr. Pinkett. Despite the bump she'd given him, a smile split his square-jawed face.

"Is everything okay?"

"Mr. Pinkett, I'm so sorry! I wasn't looking where I was going."

He waved away her apology, a strand of silver hair falling into his eyes. "Are you well, Miss Williams?"

Ash nodded and sidled over so she could see the doors, just in case Scott came barreling through. "Yeah, just in a rush."

"It's fortuitous that we ran into each other. Literally, it turns out!" His laugh was deep and infectious, and soon Ash found herself smiling in return. "I've been meaning to speak to you."

She dragged her eyes away from the doors and back to the teacher. He was much easier on the eyes.

"I've been wondering why you didn't take honors English this year."

The last thing she needed right now was a lecture about not meeting her potential. Her words came through gritted teeth, though she tried to mask it behind a smile. "Sorry, Mr. Pinkett. Nothing personal, it's just that—"

Mr. Pinkett leaned closer, so close she could smell the woodsy scent of his aftershave. She could see herself in his dilating pupils. "You see, I miss having you in class," he breathed.

Did he just sniff me?

"You've grown into such a beautiful, remarkable young woman." His hand twitched like it longed to touch her.

Ash was so shocked, her feet rooted to the floor.

His eyes strafed side to side without his head moving. Like he'd just remembered where they were, his hand fell from where it had hovered inches from her face. "You know, I'd love to tutor you. Perhaps we can meet one-on-one? I know it's Spring Break, but I'm free now. I don't live far from here."

She worked her mouth, but no words came out. His hand lifted again like he was going to caress her cheek. Her skin crawled like it was trying to escape his touch. Finally, she forced the words through her tight throat.

"Is that Principal Mancini?"

Mr. Pinkett blinked a few times like he just awakened from a dream, and his head followed where she was pointing. She didn't wait for him to respond. She stepped around him and fled the food court.

20

Ash could barely muster the energy to walk up the stairs to her bedroom where she knew Sam was fretfully waiting for her return. All she wanted to do was curl up and sleep for a week.

No, first I want to shower, then sleep for a week.

Sam was pacing along the strip of sunlight streaming in from the windows. He looked like he'd been punched in the gut. Seeing her, he didn't waste any time. "What happened?"

She toppled onto her bed like a felled tree.

"Well? What happened? Did you find Veronica?" His voice warred between excitement and terror.

The bedsprings squeaked under her. "No problem." Her terse response got the expected result, and she smiled. Giving Sam a hard time always rejuvenated her.

"What do you mean 'no problem?'" He practically vibrated with tension.

She sat up and shrugged. "No problem."

"You were gone for hours."

"You can't rush these things, Samael."

He deflated. "It took four hours to convince her?"

"Well, no. It only took about ten minutes to convince her to give you a shot."

"What did you do the rest of the time?"

The question bounced around her head. Part of her wanted to—needed to—tell him what happened with Scott and Mr. Pinkett. Unshed tears stung her eyes, but she clamped down on the bubbling emotion. Sam was kind and gentle, but he carried a darkness within him. Buried deep, he only let it out when he was protecting someone he loved. The last time she'd seen it was on their eighth-grade trip to Arkham when some creeper on the subway grabbed Ash's ass. It took two chaperones and a morning commuter to pull Sam off the guy. That had put a stop to their end-of-year field trip to the big city. The assistant principal called Sam's mom, and when Alice got there, Ash insisted on leaving with them.

Alice had been distraught when she discovered what her son had done, but that only lasted until Ash told her Sam had been protecting her. The mom didn't exactly say she was proud that her son assaulted someone, but Ash remembered the look on Alice's face, the pride. Then Alice took them out for a night on the town.

That was a long time ago, when Sam was still a skinny boy, before he was serious about fitness and got jacked. Ash shuddered to think what Sam would do to Scott, and even Mr. Pinkett, if she told him. So, she didn't.

"Well, I couldn't just leave right afterwards. That would've been weird. Like I was your pimp or something." Her eyes lit up. "Hey, we could totally do that! What was that HBO show with the guy who played Two Face? Aaron Eckhart?"

Sam blew out his lips in exasperation. "You're thinking of Thomas Jane."

"Whatever, they're the same person."

"I...don't disagree, but we're not doing it."

"Come on! Instead of a washed-up teacher reliving his glory days, it could be a high school nerd realizing his potential. A nerdy boy's struggle to discover self-worth."

"Nope."

"CUMMING OF AGE, Sam. That's what we'll call it! CUMMING, Sam! Get it?" She splayed her hands like she was unveiling the car of the future to a bunch of yokels. "The Sam Dyer Story."

"I think the name's too long for a TV show."

Ash gasped, and her hands flew to her mouth, eyes wide with excitement. "*It's too long for TV.* I think we just found the title of our pilot episode!"

"Are you done?"

"Just consider it, I think *it will grow on you*." She smiled mischievously and bobbed her eyebrows.

Sam looked at her with dead eyes, face slack. "Just tell me what happened already."

She deflated and pouted. "You're no fun."

"Details. Now." He was getting frustrated, and despite her teasing, she understood. He had spent years admiring Veronica from afar. Ash had encouraged him to say something, but he was just so damned shy, not to mention stubborn, and nothing ever came of it.

"Okay, okay. I'll tell you what happened, just chill. I found her at the mall hanging out with Amber and some girls from Dunwich."

"That's all very fascinating, but what about *me*?"

Ash rolled her eyes. "God, you're so vain."

"Need I remind you what's at stake here?"

"Fine. At first, she said no." Ash held up her hand to stop Sam before he said anything. "She said you blew her off the other day when she asked you to the dance."

"She didn't ask me to the dance."

"She said she did."

"No, she asked me if I was excited for the dance."

Ash gave him *The Look*. The look you gave to boys when they were being utterly clueless. "That's the same thing."

"In what world is that the same thing?"

Ash held up her hands to stop the conversation before they could go off on another tangent. "I don't have the time to educate you on how much a bonehead you are."

"Thank god," he muttered.

"We'd be here all night." He growled, and she smiled sweetly at him. "But that wasn't the hang up. She said you gave off total SDE."

"What's SDE?"

"Small dick energy."

"Is that... Is that a thing?"

"Totes. But don't worry, I cleared it up and told her what you're packing."

Sam's face drained of color and then, like a mood ring on a bipolar toddler, scarlet with embarrassment. "WHAT?"

"Well, not like *Konstantin* big. I mean, there's a reason his nickname is 'Bear' and it isn't because of how hairy he is, if you know what I mean."

Sam sounded like he was gagging on a chicken bone. "How would you know!?"

"Oh, please. He's making his way through the upperclassmen. And he's such a perv, he'll show it to anyone."

That derailed Sam's train of thought. "Wait, what do you mean upperclass*men*?"

"I'm pretty sure *technically* he goes both ways, but he's pretty entrenched on the other team. At this point, I think he's banged half the soccer team."

Sam pinched the bridge of his nose. "We're getting off-track again. What do you mean you 'told her what I'm packing'?"

"You know..." She gestured at him.

"No, I don't know."

"You know...that you're carrying heat. That you're taller lying down. That—"

"How would YOU know?"

Ash paused and gave him one of her best eye rolls. "Sam, do I need to remind you of the whole bit we just did about Aaron Eckhart?"

"Thomas Jane."

"They're the same person! The point is that we already established that you're a fucking tripod. Hell, even my neighbor's kid knows about it now."

"First, it's too soon to be joking about that. Second, that's...circumstantial."

"This isn't a courtroom, Sam."

"You know what I mean! It's...speculation...third-hand, whatever. It's not like you've seen it, so why would you tell Veronica that?"

An expression of shocked incredulity contorted her face. "Seriously, Sam? After all the times you spent the night, you don't think I noticed your morning wood? After all the times you went swimming in my pool? Those swim trunks are *super* thin."

Sam's mouth fell open, and his hands dropped to his cover himself like he was wearing the trunks now. "You said they were fine!"

"Yeah, *fine.*" She looked him up and down with exaggerated lasciviousness. Sam gasped and turned beet red. "Don't be such a baby. Remember when Rhonda Miller gave you a handy at her birthday party?" Sam didn't respond, just stared at her in horror. She flourished her hands toward his nether region again. "That was two weeks after I bought those trunks for you. And why are you complaining? It seems like every time I buy you clothes you get lucky. Now…are you done being such a little bitch so we can get down to business?"

They spent the next hour talking about what Sam would do on the date. Where to go for dinner, what to order, and what to say. Despite his recent run-in with Mrs. Murray, Sam wasn't *experienced*, so she tried to give tips on what to do *after* dinner, but he kept plugging his ears until she stopped talking. Oh well, he'd figure it out.

More likely Veronica will figure it out for him.

After she'd given him strict instructions on what to wear and what to do with his hair, Sam left to get ready.

After the frenetic ball of nerves that was her best friend left, Ash dropped onto her bed and stared at the ceiling. She wondered if she should have told him the truth. That it hadn't been that easy to convince Veronica to go on a date with him. It took a little more than she'd let on. Veronica may have a reputation, but she wasn't a total slut.

THE ACCURSED

Sam had really pissed Veronica off when he didn't ask her to the dance. So, Ash had to explain that while Sam may look like a man on the outside, inside he was really just another dumb boy with no idea how to talk to women. She also told Veronica that Sam was the kindest and most considerate guy she knew. That he always thought about his friends, and in all the years she'd known him, he'd never once forgotten her birthday and had even willingly gone to every chick flick she'd ever wanted to watch at the theater.

Then there was the time in Arkham where he almost beat that creeper to death... A shiver had run around the table of girls when Ash told that story. Yes, it was the 21st century, and they were supposed to be strong, independent women who didn't need no man, but there was just something about a protector that was just so panty-meltingly hot.

After a moment of silence, one girl from Dunwich volunteered to go on a date with Sam if Veronica didn't agree. But Veronica turned to Ash and had said something that pulled the rug out from Ash's feet.

"If he's so perfect, then why aren't you with him instead of Randy?"

In retrospect, Ash shouldn't have spent so long extolling all Sam's virtues. She should have talked about how he was a terrible cook, that he complained when she made him break his nutrition plan, or that he was woefully uninformed about women. But it was too late for that.

Veronica's question was harder to answer than it should have been. She should have been able to say *because I'm not interested, because he's my best friend, or because he's basically my father's son*.

But those excuses weren't good enough.

"Because he likes *you*," was what she said, and she almost choked on the words.

Yeah, maybe she should have told Sam that Veronica took some convincing, but the Lord knows the guy needed a confidence boost. Even with Veronica's proclivities, she and Sam hooking up tonight wasn't a done deal.

But we need it to be.

Ash groaned and rolled over, burying her head in a massive pile of pillows. Since Veronica had asked that damned question, it was all Ash could think about. She barely remembered saying goodbye and leaving the food court. She had told Sam that she hung out with the girls for a while, but the truth was she spent the time walking and mulling over the question.

Why hadn't she and Sam ever hooked up? On paper, he seemed like the perfect guy. God knew she dated worse, much worse. Ash had practically made her way through the rugby team. And the basketball team. She'd like to say that she had a thing for jocks, but she'd dated a handful of band geeks, too.

So why haven't we ever dated?

The thought sent a thrill of fear through her. If they ever dated, what would happen if they ever broke up? Sam seemed like the perfect guy, but let's be honest, Ash was a mess.

I mean, look at my track record. My longest relationship by far has been with Randy. And *that* wasn't saying much.

A more supportive part of her psyche rose in her defense. *It's not just my fault, though. What do you expect when you date some of the biggest jerks in school?*

Hmm. Maybe there was something to that. Maybe she hadn't dated Sam because he wasn't a jerk. If she created a wordcloud listing the personality traits of her former paramours, "douchebag" would probably be the most prominent characteristic.

Yikes, Ash.

This was why she didn't like introspection. She was much more comfortable doing and not thinking. It was much more fun and didn't leave you feeling like shit or questioning your life choices.

With a concerted effort, she shunted aside whatever character development epiphany she was verging on and got back to what was originally torturing her.

Did she want to date Sam?

The two-hour-long walk hadn't yielded any answers, and she wasn't any closer to answering it now.

Walking up the steps to her room was one of the hardest things she had ever done. She wanted to tell Sam that she struck out with Veronica, but that would have doomed her dad, Alice, Judy...and everyone else. Because there were people, a lot more. While Sam was getting the car ready at the hospital, she overheard Dottie talking to the nurses about the influx of coma patients.

Sam already had enough to worry about, so she hadn't told him. The last thing they needed was for him to hit it off with Veronica and strike out because of performance anxiety.

Her eyes found the painting across the room. It was finally on the wall where she could see it from bed. For the first time since discovering it at Heavenly Treasures, she didn't find it pretty. The two lovers embracing didn't fill her with the thrill of love, nor did it send shivers of anticipatory delight when she thought about Randy holding her like that.

The urge to toss it out the window was almost too strong to fight. Almost.

There may not be a curse. All this could be for nothing, and she could be spending her dad's last hours playing matchmaker for the clueless guy she might be in love with and the girl that *he* was in love with.

She almost laughed. For the first time in her life, she had found not one but two things she feared: destroying the painting that might be the key to saving her family...and confronting her feelings for her best friend.

21

The wheel of the Tercel bumped against the curb. Sam cringed, hoping Veronica didn't notice. Unfortunately, she was standing about four feet away, so there was no way she missed it. He hurriedly threw the car into park and jumped out.

Unfortunately, he didn't get far. He struggled against the seatbelt for an embarrassing amount of time before realizing the problem—him. He was the problem. Taking a deep breath, he reached down and pressed the button to unbuckle, then executed a stately exit from the beat-up Toyota.

Success.

Sam rounded the car and got his first look at Veronica. His stomach lurched, and then his shoe caught the curb—that same, cock-blocking curb—and he almost sprawled to the sidewalk. He did a little half-stumble, half-windmill dance before regaining his balance.

Veronica wore a skirt, a pair of red Chuck Taylor's, and a white top that exposed an amazing amount of cleavage. Her hair hung in a tail on the side of her head, her brunette locks flowing down her shoulder in curly ringlets.

"You look... Wow."

A smile blossomed on her lips, and she ran her hands from her waist down her skirt. "Good answer. You don't look half bad yourself."

He made a mental note to thank Ash for the outfit.

"Thanks. Ready to go?"

"Think you can manage the curb this time?"

Blushing and mumbling something incoherent—even to him—he opened the passenger door for her. Stepping back, he nearly collided with her. "Sorry, I was just—"

Surprise flitted across her face, no doubt because of his clumsiness, then she regained her composure and smiled again, this time with no hint of teasing. "Thank you."

Making sure she was tucked safely in the car before closing the door, he rushed around the back of the car—stumbling off the curb again—but made it to the driver seat without additional injury. The obstinate seatbelt wouldn't release. He pulled on it five or twelve times until, chastising himself silently and trying not to glance at Veronica, he pulled slowly. The belt relented and did as it was designed to. He sent a timid smile her way and put the car in gear, thankful he left the car running. The Tercel had started on the first try on the way over, so it was statistically impossible that it would do so twice in a row.

Like just about everywhere in Elsbury, it only took four minutes to drive to the restaurant. At the Mountains of Munchies featured cuisine from no fewer than eight cultures and had a bustling take-and-bake pizza bar. It was the fanciest restaurant in town that he could afford.

The hostess led them to a table as soon as they walked in. There was an awkward moment when he and Veronica both attempted to pull out her chair, both vying for and stepping back from it a few times before Veronica let him do it for her.

Her hair brushed against his arm as he scooted the chair in for her. "Looks like we have the place mostly to ourselves."

"Monday nights probably aren't too popular for diners." Frazzled-looking parents and their spawn occupied three other tables in the restaurant. Sam laughed louder than her joke warranted.

The hostess filled their water glasses and left them without uttering a single word. The neat text on the menu swirled in his vision.

Jesus, am I having a stroke? The ice rattled in his glass as he brought it to his lips for a gulp, and a small wave of ice-cold water splashed on his pants. Luckily, Veronica's eyes were on her own menu, so he didn't think she noticed.

"So how was your day?" Was his voice higher pitched than normal?

Veronica didn't take her eyes off the menu. "*Sooo* boring. I hoped Spring Break would be more exciting, but with all these accidents, everyone's scared to do anything, and it's all they want to talk about."

"What accidents?"

A small frown creased her pretty brow. "You know, all these people falling into comas. Where have you been?"

It was like his chair fell out from underneath him. He'd been so wrapped up with everything going on with Mr. Williams and his mom and Judy and trying to help Ash that he hadn't heard anything. He wasn't big on reading the news in the first place, and with school out for Spring Break, he didn't have access to the rumor mill.

There are more people in comas? "Do you know someone who's gotten sick?"

"Ugh, yes. My neighbor got sick this morning. My mom was totally freaking out. I don't know why, Mrs. Caswell is like a hundred years old and went to the emergency room like six times last month."

"Wow, that's terrible." Sam was only half listening. He pulled his cell phone out of his pocket, keeping it below the table while he texted Ash.

More people are falling into comas!

He put his phone in his lap and smiled at Veronica. Their waiter arrived a moment later. He had graduated a couple years prior. Duncan or Brady or something like that. He had an impossibly square jaw, dimples, and a more-on-top faded haircut.

"Hi," he said in a rich baritone, nodding at Sam but saving his smile for Veronica. "Welcome to At the Mountains of Munchies. My name's Braden, and I'll be happy to service *you* tonight."

Sam rolled his eyes and opened his mouth to ask what the specials were when his phone vibrated.

Ash's response was only three emojis, followed by a short sentence.

Peach. Eggplant. Water splash. *Get in there already!*

Veronica's laughter caught his attention, and he jerked his eyes away from the screen. Her eyes and smile were aimed at the waiter. Sam coughed.

The beefcake waiter turned to him. "What can I get ya, champ?"

"I'll have the chicken tacos, please." Ash had told him to order either oysters or fish tacos, but he was pretty sure she had been joking. With Ash, it was hard to tell. Plus, he didn't care for seafood.

Braden acknowledged the order with practiced disinterest and turned back to Veronica. "And what would you like to eat tonight?"

THE ACCURSED

Veronica met Sam's gaze, and with a smirk, she ordered the eggplant parmesan. Braden wasn't happy with the shift her attention had taken. He snapped his little black book closed and walked away brusquely.

The predatory grin Veronica shot Sam sent blood rushing to two very different parts of his body, one above the table and one that was—thankfully—hidden below it.

The ice in his glass rattled like a maraca, and he managed to take a sip without spilling half a gallon on himself. Veronica's flirting with the waiter seemed like it was the end of any chance he had at stopping the curse—that was the euphemism he was using to keep his mind off what he needed to do—but things were suddenly looking up.

Maybe she's actually *interested*.

Braden sauntered by and dropped off a basket of breadsticks. "I hope you find my breadstick is just the right size for you." He winked at Sam's date, and Veronica rewarded the jackass with a giggle.

While they talked, Sam glanced down at his phone and sent an SOS to Ash.

Not going well. Himbo waiter got game!

Braden took his perfect hair left, but he didn't go far. He leaned against the bar a dozen feet away and made no attempt to pretend like he wasn't looking at their table, looking right at Veronica.

Sam fumed. *This isn't going well. I have to do something.*

To her credit, Veronica didn't seem ready to throw in the towel on their date. She carried the conversation, and Sam did his best to keep up his side of the conversation, but with Braden hovering at the edge of his vision, he didn't think he was doing too well.

Sam's phone buzzed in his lap.

"Is that yours?"

He shook his head. "Nope, not mine." He waited until she was taking a drink of her iced tea and read the text.

Say something funny, dipshit! Don't fuck it up!

Gritting his teeth, Sam shoved the phone back into his pocket. Ash was no help. When he looked back up, Veronica had turned away, her lips pursed like she was mad.

Fuck, she probably saw me texting. Say something!

"Did you hear that Aaron Eckhart and Thomas Jane are the same person?"

No, asshole! Not like that!

The look she gave him was not promising. "What?"

"You know, the guy who played...um...Two Dicks. No, I mean, he was the teacher in that show who became a gigolo. Same guy!"

Veronica looked at him like he'd just ripped a long, wet fart. Braden chose that moment to bring their food out.

"Chicken tacos for the big guy, and eggplant parmesan for—" He must have picked up on the awkwardness floating around the table like a swarm of mosquitoes. He sent a discerning glance at Sam and then turned back to Veronica. "Here ya go. You know, I get off in about half an hour if you wanted to do something once you're done hanging out with your"—he spared Sam a quick glance as if to say, *Sorry, dude, but you shot your shot, now it's time to step aside*—"little brother."

Veronica gave the waiter an appraising look. "I'll keep it in mind."

Sam's heart fell into his stomach. *I fucked it up.* He looked down at his tacos. Sam loved the tacos here. At the Mountains of Munchies was the second best TexMex restaurant in town—and they were the third best Thai and very best Italian restaurant—but for once, his mouth wasn't watering.

THE ACCURSED

These are not the tacos I'm supposed to be eating tonight. He tried to meet Veronica's gaze to see if there was any hope to salvage the night, but her eyes were tracking the waiter. *Ash is going to kill me.*

"You know what, Sam?" Veronica asked, beginning the preamble to what Sam knew was coming next. "I don't think this date is going very well."

22

Ash fidgeted restlessly and looked at her phone for the thousandth time. Still nothing. She exhaled a deep breath and tried to push all the fear, desperation, and anxiety out of her with that one breath. It didn't help.

It took Sam all day to get ready for his big date, so she'd spent the day at the hospital visiting Dad, Alice, and Judy—all the adults she considered family. She was there until the night shift nurse kicked her out. Everyone was stable, the nurse had said, and there was nothing Ash could do for them pacing the hospital's halls. So she went home and paced in her room.

Judy getting sick had been bad enough. She was one of Ash's oldest friends and one of the few remaining links she had to her mother. Then when Dad had his accident, Ash thought she had lost everything. Judy was one thing...but her dad was *everything*.

She didn't know, hadn't consciously understood, how important Alice was to her. They had a tight bond, but she hadn't realized how deep it ran. When her father got sick, all she wanted was for Alice to hold her and tell her everything was going to be okay. And then she was gone, too.

Not gone, she reminded herself. She was wrung out. She'd cried so much over the last few days.

And now... Sam. Samael Fucking Dyer.

Her brain burned, and her stomach ached like she swallowed a brick.

Is this what jealousy feels like? She couldn't remember ever being jealous. Well, she remembered when Lisa Herrington got boobs in the eighth grade and all the boys paid attention to *her*. Ash was definitely jealous then. But that was different.

There was a time, as kids, when she and Sam talked about getting married. In the same way they talked about being a prince, a knight, a princess, they talked about getting married and living together forever. Their parents even joked about how they were destined to be together. The girl Williams and Dyer boy, destined to unite their families in wedlock. But as time went on and they grew up, they stopped playing husband-and-wife. No romantic feelings ever sprouted.

Sam had girlfriends before. Nothing serious, of course, but Ash was never jealous of them. Even when he got the handjob from Rhonda Miller that summer, she hadn't been jealous. The only thing she remembered thinking was: *Rhonda Miller? Really?*

Now, though... Now, she was wracked with...something. Jealousy? Anger? Sadness?

She pictured Sam and Veronica at dinner, laughing, making eyes at each other. *Knowing Veronica, she's probably giving him a blowjob under the table.* Part of her wanted to scream. Another part of her wanted to vomit.

THE ACCURSED

You have a boyfriend, for god's sake! And Sam had been pining for Veronica for literally years. Who was Ash to stop him from being with her? Now, of all times, when so many people were in danger?

Even if people weren't in danger, she and Randy had been dating for nearly a year. They'd made out in front of Sam. She had told Sam *eeeeeeverything*. All the details of what they'd done with each other, to each other. To do that, to share those intimate details, and then have the gall to try to stop him now... Who did she think she was?

Even after the silent conversation with herself, she wanted to scream. Why did she feel so shitty?

When Sam texted her about the other people being sick, she knew she had to get his mind back on track. She typed up the text of suggestive emojis and would rather have chewed her arm off than send it.

When he texted that the date wasn't going well, her stomach did flipflops. It was equal parts, "Yay! He's not going down on that slut!" and "God damnit, Dyer, you better take the hot dog bus to taco town!" Never had she been so conflicted.

"Text me, you fucker!" No matter how many times she screamed it at her phone, no texts came through. She *needed* to know what was going on. Knowing was better than wondering. That was what she told herself, at least. She squeezed the phone and shook it.

As if in response, the phone vibrated, causing her heart to lurch. But it was only an email. Growling, she threw the traitorous phone onto the bed. She didn't want to see it anymore, but at the same time, she wanted to refresh the screen four times per second, waiting for—and dreading—the text that would let her know the curse was over.

Ash finally gave in and retrieved the treacherous device. Still no texts from Sam or Veronica. The knot in her stomach loosened. Slightly.

The next hour was possibly the most excruciating she'd ever lived through, and she used to be in the drama club.

Finally, after hours of pacing, trying not to pace, and thinking about pacing, she fell into a fitful sleep, her eyes wet and burning from staring at the small bright screen.

Yeah, that was why. The brightly lit screen.

23

THE DOOR BOOMED UNDER her rapid-fire assault. If Ash hadn't learned long ago never to barge into a teenage boy's room, she'd have kicked the door down. The light trickling in from the hallway window was pale and watery. She could *not* believe she was up that early, especially during Spring Break. It had been a looong time since *she* woke *Sam* up.

She pounded on the door again. On the third knock, Sam answered, looking like how she felt. Dark, bloodshot eyes, hair astray, he stood in the doorway wearing nothing but athletic boxer briefs and a confused expression.

"Wha—what's wrong? What time is it?"

Ash stormed into his bedroom, head on a swivel, but she saw nothing out of the ordinary. It was still an 18-year-old boy's room, so it wasn't exactly clean, but there definitely wasn't a teenage girl hiding anywhere.

"Put some pants on, Samael."

Sam paused rubbing the sleep out of his eyes to look down. He started and hunted for something to put on. He stumbled to the dresser and nearly fell over pulling on a pair of gray sweatpants.

Her pulse slowed a bit, but not by much. "Where is she?"

"Where is...who?" Sam collapsed back onto his bed with a jaw-cracking yawn.

"What do you mean 'where is who'? Where is Veronica? What happened last night? Why didn't you text me?" After each rapid-fire question, she took a step closer to him. "I've been waiting to hear from you all night, Sam Dyer. I called the hospital this morning, and there hasn't been any change with Dad, Alice, or Judy.

"*What the fuck happened?*"

"Whoa, whoa. Slow down. I just woke up."

Ash's eyes burned with intensity, not sure if she was going to scream, or cry, or both. She opened her mouth to say something, closed it, then took a deep breath. "What. Happened. With. Veronica?"

Sam buried his face into a pillow. "It didn't go according to plan." His voice was hollow and devoid of emotion.

"What do you mean? I set everything up for you. It was a done deal. All you had to do was seal it. If there ever was a sure thing, Veronica Chambers is it." She sat on the bed, nudging him until he made room for her to sit. "*Something* happened. You've been incommunicado all night."

"I mean *nothing happened*. Nothing was ever going to happen. It just wasn't... It just wasn't right, okay?"

A fusion of emotions boiled through her. Anger. Confusion. Relief.

"But...our parents..."

"I know!" Sam raged, pushing himself off the bed and starting to pace. "I'm a fucking loser, okay? Is that what you want to hear? I'm pathetic. I needed my best friend to get me a date with the easiest girl in school, and I still couldn't deliver."

Now, it was her turn to erupt. "Now isn't the time for self-pity. We need to figure out what to do. Where did you leave things with Veronica? Can we salvage this?"

"It's time for Plan B." He looked at her with an expression that she couldn't decipher. There was a silent, pregnant moment between them while they stared at each other.

Ash wanted to open her mouth and spew out everything. To vent about how fucking scared she was that they were going to lose the last of their parents. About how pissed she was at Scott and Mr. Pinkett. She wanted to confide in him how confused she'd been about him—about *them*. The words burbled up like a sneeze she couldn't stop. The moment stretched and stretched. She could see that he felt it, too, that there was something left unspoken hovering in the air between them... Then the moment snapped, falling apart.

She was a coward.

Ash didn't let herself dwell on her own shortcomings. Now wasn't the time for self-loathing, what-ifs, or maybes. Not when her dad's life was on the line.

"Where are you going?"

"Plan B," she called, closing the bathroom door behind her.

In less than a minute, she was back in the bedroom. Sam looked up from the bed. "What was that about?"

"Twat shot," she explained, opening up her text messages with Randy.

"WHAT?"

"It's like a dick pic but with vaginas."

Sam looked like he was going to be sick. "Ash, you—you can't send that to Randy. W-what if he shares it with someone?"

"Relax, I'm not really showing much. Just enough to let his imagination run wild."

"It's still not a great idea."

"It doesn't matter!" Her voice was sharper than intended, but she couldn't think about that now. "What matters is curing our parents and everyone else who's hurt. Our discomfort or feelings don't mean shit right now."

Sam hung his head, and she almost apologized for the barb. She didn't mean for it to come across as a jab at his failure to bang Veronica.

But she didn't apologize. Because the truth was, regardless of her feelings for him—whatever the hell they were—she was pissed that he couldn't set aside his bullshit long enough to stick his wand in Veronica's Chamber of Secrets.

"I thought Randy was on vacation."

Ash smiled, but it didn't reach her eyes. "Once he sees that, he'll be on the first flight home. I guarantee it." Sam looked confused, so she clarified. "I'm telling him I'm ready to put out."

His expression morphed, shifting from confusion to what looked like nausea. She could relate but didn't let it deter her from what needed doing. It was already Tuesday, and they were running out of time.

It was time to end this.

24

Nurse Jessica Strong's shoes squeaked on the polished tile floor. It didn't matter which shoes she wore or how she altered her gait, they squealed with every step. It drove her absolutely bonkers. Luckily, her patients didn't seem to mind. To be fair, it was hard to be annoyed by a sound you couldn't even hear. The residents of Twisting Oaks Nursing Home were a hard-of-hearing bunch. She had been told by the veteran nurses that the noise would soon fade into the background, and soon, she wouldn't even notice it anymore.

Working the night shift made the squeak worse. The place was so quiet; every sound was amplified like it was shouted into an echo chamber. She couldn't do anything about that, though. Newbies always got stuck with the least desirable shifts.

Most people thought of nursing homes as a place where old folk went to die. Lonely, boring places where Wednesday morning bingo was the highlight of the week. That was partly true. Twisting Oaks was the last stop for most of the residents. A few were there to recuperate from acute issues that families or friends couldn't handle on their own. Those residents were the lucky ones. Those got to go home once they convalesced. The rest were permanent fixtures.

"Permanent" wasn't *exactly* the right word. The life expectancy of a new resident was less than two years. Jessica hadn't lost anyone yet, but her coworkers assured her it was definitely a *when* and not an *if*. She dreaded the day she lost her first patient.

Jessica hadn't expected to grow so close to the residents. Prior to her interview for the position she had never been in a nursing home, so she didn't know what to expect. Most of what she knew came from movies and TV shows; the residents were comatose, vegetative, or bat-shit crazy out of their minds.

The truth, as was often the case, was much stranger than fiction.

Nursing homes, at least the good ones like Twisting Oaks, kept the residents active, entertained, and engaged. Not that the residents of Twisting Oaks needed any help with that. There was always something going on. Birthday parties, holiday parties, celebrations of life. If there was an occasion, the residents were celebrating it. Her first week on the job they'd thrown a party for Sandy passing a large kidney stone. The cake decorations were…terrifying.

Any chance to throw a party. They also organized dances, ice cream socials, and field trips to nearby venues like the park, library, or movie theater. And that didn't include all the outside organizations that came to visit. Boy Scouts and Girl Scouts, and some local schools to perform plays or put on talent shows for the residents. And then, of course, there were the most popular visitors: the four-legged kind. The local Humane Society brought animals in once a week to visit.

And all that was just the events that happened out in the open. What most people didn't know—and probably never, ever, wanted to think about—was that the prevalence of STIs in nursing homes was eight times higher than the national average. *Old people be getting it on!*

THE ACCURSED

Since Jessica had started, her blissful ignorance of post-septuagenarian sexual habits had been shattered.

Many residents were injured during their tenure. Poor eyesight and fragile bodies were a recipe for orthopedic disaster. What most people didn't know was that many—*so* many!—of those injuries were actually caused by bedroom acrobatics gone awry. If anyone ever reviewed the medical records, they'd see that the cause of most orthopedic injuries were chalked up to trips and falls. But that was just what the nursing staff put on the paperwork.

People who worked in the retail, food service, or medical industries often talked about how the moon cycle affected the craziness of the population. Jessica didn't know if she believed in any of that, but the new moon was a couple days away, and the residents of Twisting Oaks Nursing Home were busier than usual. Getting busier than normal, that is. The inhabitants shuffled, wheeled, and were rolled into each other's rooms for late-night rendezvous.

Once the initial surprise passed, Jessica realized she didn't mind at all. It kept things interesting, and she was genuinely happy her patients found comfort in each other's arms. As happy as she was for the amorous residents, that didn't mean she enjoyed walking in on two of them going at it like wild animals. Doing the late-night medication run was often an awkward and horrifying experience.

The med cart clattered as she pushed it into its home in the medication closet and locked the wheels. She took a moment to rest her head on the cool stainless-steel metal top and congratulated herself on navigating through yet another night of coital escapades. After three weeks of doing med runs, she had the process down. The key was to give plenty of warning before opening any doors.

She spent the next twenty minutes cleaning and prepping the med cart for the next round. Not every nurse took the time to do it, but it was always easier for her starting off with a fresh one, so she made it a habit. When she finally left the closet, the pneumatic arm sucked the door into place, and the lock beeped. The last step of the med run procedure was to make sure the lock engaged properly, so Jess gave the door a yank. Satisfied, she headed down the hallway. It was late, just past midnight. She did one last round through the hallways to make sure all was well. By that hour, the residents had finished their trysts and shuffled back to their own rooms, so it was all quiet.

"How'd it go?" Maggie popped her gum and leaned back in the ergonomic chair at the nurses' station. A long bank of monitors and speakers crammed the countertop behind her. If something went awry with any of the monitored patients, or if any resident called for assistance, one of those devices would notify them.

"All the Romeos and Juliets are back in bed." She and Maggie shared a laugh. Jessica pulled her lunch pail from the tiny fridge under the counter and melted into a chair. It was the first time she had sat in hours, and her feet made their protests clear. Keeping up with the residents, even at a quarter of their age, took a lot out of her.

Maggie rolled her chair over to bump against Jessica's. "Hey, do you mind if..."

Jessica swallowed a spoonful of yogurt. "Didn't get any sleep again today?"

"What can I say? The newlywed life is a busy time."

"I can't even get a guy to sleep with me once, and here you've got one who can't keep his hands off you."

Maggie barked a laugh. "Trust me, sister. It took time. You gotta lay the groundwork before you reap the rewards."

"That's all I'm looking for. Someone to *lay the groundwork*." They shared another laugh, and Jessica nodded toward the dormitories. "Go ahead."

Maggie logged out of the monitoring system so Jess could sign in and waved over her shoulder. Maggie walked across the hall and slipped into a vacant room. There were a lot of regulations for running a nursing home. Sleeping on the job was technically violating nurse-to-patient ratio regs, but once Jessica started on the night shift, she soon found out that it was one of those things that happened that everyone pretended didn't.

So far Jess had kept her sleeping to quick naps during scheduled breaks, but she was young, unmarried, and didn't have children or any kind of social life. She didn't mind covering for her coworker, especially when things were quiet. She didn't mind working through her lunch so Maggie could sleep. It wasn't like she could go anywhere during lunch, anyway. She pulled up the Netflix app on her phone and pressed play on something from her queue to keep her awake.

Even when everyone was supposed to be asleep, the night shift at a nursing home wasn't idle. Medications had to be dispensed, and residents needed help going to the bathroom or shifting positions. Old bodies ached easily, and bedsores were a major concern for some of their less mobile residents. New meds wreaked havoc on circadian rhythms, and residents' meds were *constantly* getting changed.

That night was no different. While Maggie slept, Jess took bites of her lunch and watched Jackie Chan kick a bunch of gangsters' asses between all the calls. Two to four o'clock was the quietest time. Despite all the hubbub and her efforts, the quiet lulled Jessica to sleep.

She didn't wake until she heard the screaming. The chair nearly toppled as she jerked awake. Maggie burst from the vacant room, wide awake. She'd been on night shift for nearly a decade and was well accustomed to waking quickly.

Hallway A echoed with another scream. They rounded the corner together and saw Roberta, one of their more spry patients, dressed in a long periwinkle robe. She stood in Darnell's doorway, her hands clasped over her mouth, cane forgotten on the floor. No doubt there for their daily coffee and game of checkers. Jessica and Maggie's shoes sounded like an orchestra of baby birds as they rushed past the distraught woman, stopping dead in their tracks. More experienced nurses liked to pretend they'd seen it all, but even Maggie was speechless.

Darnell was an early riser. He may be old, but he prided himself on his dapper appearance, treating each day and each outfit like it was his last.

That morning, Darnell was not wearing one of his favorite suits. He didn't have a fresh flower in his jacket pocket, no silken cravat, no gleaming cufflinks at his wrists. Instead, he lay in bed, in a pair of flannel pajamas favored by so many grandpas. His chest wasn't moving, but that wasn't surprising.

Maggie and Jessica hesitated for the briefest of moments before their training kicked in, and they rushed to check his vitals.

"Gloves." Maggie's pair of purple nitrile gloves were already on her hands. Jessica fumbled to get her own out of the pocket of her scrubs. Her hands shook.

THE ACCURSED

Twisted Oaks wasn't a hospital. Yes, they still went through a lot of gloves, but they didn't wear them for every little thing, especially not on the night shift. The complicated and messy things were supposed to happen during the day shift. The night shift motto was "Keep 'em alive till 7:05." Most nights it was med runs and helping residents walk to the bathroom. It was a rare shift when Jess went through two pairs.

But she didn't argue Maggie's order. Not once she saw Darnell's skin. "What the..."

With an adroit motion honed by years of experience, Maggie slipped her stethoscope off her neck and into position. Jessica's already high estimation of Maggie leaped up a few notches when the older nurse only hesitated a single instant before pressing her fingers to Darnell's carotid artery and checking for a pulse.

Holes pocked his dark skin and bored through the flannel and blankets alike like he'd been eaten through by worms, and he looked like he hadn't had a sip of water for weeks. What little skin they could see was covered in a dark...*something*.

"Is this...bark?" Jessica hesitated to touch it. It was the color and texture of wet oak bark, split and cracked like the surface of a desiccated mud puddle.

"Call it in!"

Jessica lifted the phone, her fingers punching in the number she'd memorized before her first shift.

Neither said it, but they knew it was no use. Darnell was dead. Once the paramedics arrived and Jessica and Maggie were able to start their morning rounds, they discovered everyone else was, too.

25

It took longer than expected for Randy to get home. In less than 24 hours, the new moon would rise over Elsbury, and it would be too late. Ash fidgeted from foot to foot as the Uber crawled up Randy's driveway, her stomach twisting into a knot as her boyfriend got closer and closer. She plastered on her best smile. Randy looked good in his slacks, blazer, and polo. He stepped out of the car and opened his arms.

Running to him, she buried her face in his chest. His cologne tickled her nose, but a genuine smile replaced the fake one from a moment ago. It was the first hug they'd shared since her father got sick, and Randy's muscular arms were warm and comforting. He enveloped her, and she melted into the embrace. She took a long, shaky breath and sneezed when his cologne invaded her sinuses.

"I knew you couldn't hold out much longer, babe. No one can resist this for long." He splayed the panels of his blazer out and wiggled his hips, a lascivious smile on his face.

The instinct to slap him reared up, but she fought it down. After everything that had happened, the first thing he thought to say to her was she couldn't hold out much longer?

Now's not the time, she reminded herself. She clamped down on the anger welling inside her and smiled, tugging on his blazer and leading him up the steps.

"Whatever's gotten into you, I like it."

The decorative panels on the door dug into her back as he pinned her against it and kissed her, pressing his warm, hard body against hers. He smelled like Battleaxe body spray and hookers. Knowing his father's proclivities, and how Randy had never heard the word "no" growing up, it wouldn't be surprising if the Masters men spent their vacation in strip clubs. Atlantic City wasn't known for its family-friendly attractions, after all.

She nearly gagged, both at the nasal onslaught and the thought of him in a sleazy strip club. Where his hands touched her, Ash's skin crawled, and she pushed him away.

He groaned. "Not this again. You said you were ready. Look, I even brought condoms like you asked for." He pulled out a black box with gold lettering from his pocket, the letters XL emblazoned on the front.

It took all her effort to stop from rolling her eyes. Condom sizes were basically bogus, just a way for the manufacturers to bilk men's fragile egos. Their sex ed teacher demonstrated the elasticity of "normal-sized" condoms by rolling one over her entire forearm. And even if condom sizes weren't just a scam, there was no way Randy of all people needed a magnum. *Someone like Sam on the other hand...*

No! No, no, no, nope! No time for bullshit. Focus!

The flitting thought brought a smile to her face, which Randy misinterpreted for excitement and kissed her again. This time Ash got swept up in the moment, and she didn't stop Randy's hand from slipping under her blouse and cupping her breast. Guilt reared its ugly head. Here she was with Randy, getting ready to pop her cherry, and she couldn't stop thinking about Sam.

"Open the door."

Randy fumbled the keyring out of his pocket, and they stumbled over the threshold and into the entryway. The synthetic fabric of his slacks did little to hide his excitement. She let the kiss linger a little longer, then pushed him away again.

"What now?" His voice was an exasperated growl.

"Not in the hallway. I want it to be...special."

He smirked. "Don't worry about that. I'm gonna give you the Masters' special all night long."

Again, she fought to stop herself from rolling her eyes. *More empty promises.*

"I want it to be special...and definitely not where one of the maids can walk in."

"Don't worry about that. They know better than to interrupt when I'm busy."

Ignoring the implication that the staff were accustomed to him getting busy in the public spaces of the house, she pushed away from him. "I'm going to powder my nose. Why don't you...get things ready?"

"If it's powder you want, use my bathroom. You'll find everything you need in the top drawer."

Her footsteps echoed as she scampered up the wood and marble staircase. She squashed the sense that she was walking up the gallows. Randy was always trying to press party drugs on her, especially when they were fooling around. The bathroom's heavy door clunked into place, and she locked it, pressing her back against it and covering her face, trying to stop the tears. If she started crying, she wasn't sure she'd be able to stop. A scream crawled its way up her throat, but she swallowed it.

Everyone was counting on her. She *needed* to do this. But it wasn't right. Not here. Not now.

Not him...?

An angel and devil were on her shoulders, prodding her into action. All her misgivings about Randy and losing her virginity on one. All her fears of losing the people closest to her on the other.

God damn that fucking curse!

It was ridiculous to think that she was here, almost in tears in Randy's bathroom, all because of a fucking painting.

Blessing, my ass.

Her mind lingered on the painting and the blessing or curse—or whatever the fuck it was. True love, that was what it said. The blessing was supposed to be unlocked by consummating her *true love*. Even when she and Sam found the poem—spell?—she laughed at the thought of Randy being her true love. But she wasn't laughing now.

A week ago, she was nearly ready to give it up to Randy. Throughout their relationship, he'd been insistent about his interest but still patient with her. He could be sweet when he wanted to be.

Now, though... Now, she felt like a completely different person. She should be excited to have sex with her really hot boyfriend, but it felt wrong.

Could Randy be my true love? A few days ago, she didn't think so. He was just one boyfriend in a string of boyfriends like she had a Bingo card to fill up, and he was just another hot, popular high school dude she needed to fill in her row.

THE ACCURSED

Honestly, who even finds their true love in high school? And for that matter, what the fuck even was true love?

Her dad thought her mom was his true love. High school sweethearts, married young...and look where that got him. Abandoned. Betrayed by his best friend. *If that's true love, then no thanks.*

Despair threatened to sweep her away. If Randy wasn't her true love, then this was all for nothing. Dad, Alice, Judy...they were all going to die, and it would be her fault.

But if it took true love to lift the curse, and Randy *wasn't* hers, then what was she doing this for? Would she be losing her virginity for nothing? The girl who stared back in the mirror didn't have the answers. She was almost unrecognizable, same hair, same skin, eyes, and lips...but that girl wasn't her. Ash's face crumpled, and hot tears welled up. Choking back a sob, she pressed fingers against her eyes to stem the flow of tears.

I can't do it. She didn't know what would happen with the curse, with Sam, with Dad, or if Randy *was* her true love, but she knew that she wasn't ready for this.

A relieved, shuddering breath wracked her. Now that she'd decided, the grip on her chest loosened. Unshed tears still glistened on her eyelashes, but now they were tears of relief. Standing up, she began damage control on her makeup.

A chime trilled from her pocket. Probably Sam checking in on her. She unlocked the screen, and her once-blotchy complexion drained of color. Her veins flushed with ice water as she read Veronica's text.

U weren't kidding! He was a total MOUTHFUL!

The three dots at the bottom of the screen told her Veronica was still typing, but Ash powered off the phone and slammed it on the vanity top. This time when she looked in the mirror, she recognized the girl staring back at her. Determined. Angry. A girl who'd been hurt before but wouldn't let anyone push her around.

Sam *lied* to her. It didn't matter why.

Ash let the sound of smooth jazz guide her from the bathroom and back downstairs. A crystal tumbler full of amber liquid rested in Randy's hand, and he wore nothing other than his favorite robe, the red silk looking almost black in the dim light. The smirk on his face was triumphant.

26

Scotch wasn't the only thing Randy had imbibed. As she drew closer, his dilated pupils looked like they were ready to swallow her whole. He gestured to a black marble shelf behind him, a small silver platter lay atop it.

"If you didn't get enough in the bathroom, there's plenty here."

Even in the dim light, she could see the four lines of white powder on the dish, an outline of where a fifth line had been moments before. A small heap of different colored pills was piled beside the lines.

She considered taking him up on the offer, wondering if it would make what was about to happen easier, but her stomach burned with fury and betrayal. That was the only fuel she needed. "Thanks, I got plenty," she lied. As nervous as she was about having sex, she didn't want her first time to be fogged by drugs. She would just have to live with the consequences of her decisions.

The crystal tumbler clinked onto the shelf, and Randy approached, taking her into his arms. The silk robe did very little to hide his arousal. The flavor of smoky alcohol slipped into her mouth along with his tongue. Hands slid down her back and cupped her ass, squeezing hard enough she almost cried out. Instead, she bit his lip hard enough his moan of pleasure turned into a squeal of discomfort.

"Slow down, baby." His hand swiped across his lip, checking for blood. It was a short respite though, and soon, his tongue was back in her mouth. Before she knew it, her shirt was over her head, and he was fumbling at her bra.

Ash buried her doubts and tossed all her worries out the window. Swallowing her gorge, she unclasped her bra and let it slide off her arms. It wasn't the first time he'd gotten her bra off, but she appreciated his expression when he saw her tits. She slipped her hand into his robe and ran her fingers along his abs. Randy's muscles were hard and defined, even more so than S—*No! Nope, I'm not thinking about* him *right now.*

Shunting all other thoughts into a dark corner of her mind, she let her hands show her appreciation of Randy's body. Her lips kissed his chest and neck while she tugged at the knot holding his robe closed. It fell open, revealing the extent of his arousal.

Randy growled deep in his throat and squeezed her ass again before running his hands down her legs and then sliding them up her skirt. His fingertips hooked over her panties and pulled them down her legs.

She shivered, and not because of the air. They were stepping into unfamiliar territory. They'd done oral, but only a few times and always in the dark. The living room, though dimly lit, was like being onstage. She could see everything. His predatory grin, the sweat on his upper lip, even the small bead of pre-come glistening at the tip of his dick.

Still under her skirt, his hands reached around and grabbed her ass again. It was a good thing her eyes were closed because she couldn't stop her eyes from rolling. *He needs to get new material.*

THE ACCURSED

Luckily, he didn't squeeze as hard as before. He pressed his erection against her, the fabric of her skirt the only thing separating them. A soft moan escaped his lips, and he slipped a hand between her legs and up her thigh. His fingers were like a skittering spider, and her flesh rippled with revulsion.

She broke off the kiss and pushed his hand away. "Stop."

"What the fuck is wrong now? Why are you being such a tease?" A thundercloud brewed on his face.

"I'm not being a tease, it's just..."

Throwing his hands up, he stormed away from her. The decanter clinked under his angry grip, and he took a long swig, gasping and wiping his mouth. "This is fucking ridiculous! You said you were ready. I left a *sure thing* in Atlantic City, and for what? To get cock-blocked by my own girlfriend? Who do you think you are? I'm not a puppy you can lead around by its nose. You think you can dangle some tasty treat in front of me and snatch it away?"

She crossed her arms around her naked chest. "You're being an asshole."

His eyes blazed, and he stalked toward her. She'd never seen Randy angry before, and she backed away, stumbling to a stop when her legs bumped into the settee.

"You're such. A. Fucking. Tease." He was up against her now, so close she could smell the liquor on his breath. She leaned back as far as she could and struggled not to tip over, but he snaked a hand around her waist to hold them pressed together.

"Let go of me." She pushed against him, but he didn't budge. She expected a cheesy pickup line. Or even a barbed comment about how lucky she was to be dating him, how lucky that he deigned to date outside of the cheer squad, below his station. She expected him to grind himself into her or grab her ass again, some lame attempt at salvaging the arousal they'd clearly lost.

His hand came up to her face like he was going to caress her. She should have turned away, but she didn't want to give him the satisfaction of seeing her scared.

"What are you d—"

His fingers touched her lips, and she closed her mouth, cutting off the words. A sharp fingernail scratched against her top lip as Randy forced something small and hard into her mouth. Hot, salty blood coated her lips, and she tried to open her mouth to spit whatever it was out, but his hands clamped hard around her face, keeping her mouth shut tight. Whatever he put in her mouth dissolved in a flash. She jerked and hit out, but he was too strong to break free. He held her for a few more moments longer, then released her.

Ash sucked on her teeth and spat, not caring that she was making a mess on the fancy rug. She wiped her tongue on one of the throw pillows, it was rough, dusty, and tasted like ass.

"What was that? What did you give me?"

"Relax," he drawled, taking another swig from the decanter. "You'll be fine. You can thank me later."

She rushed across the room and pushed him. The decanter slipped out of his hand and shattered on the floor, liquor spraying in all directions.

"You expect me to thank you for date raping me? You fucking bastard!" She pushed again, and he staggered, hopping awkwardly to avoid the broken glass. After regaining his balance, he laughed, causing her blood to boil with renewed fury.

THE ACCURSED

"I don't need to rape you. In a couple minutes when that kicks in, I'll have to fight you off."

Her stomach roiled and churned, and she wasn't sure if it was the drugs or disgust. Looking at his smug, satisfied face, she couldn't believe she ever found him handsome.

All the assemblies and presentations she was forced to sit through said inducing vomiting wasn't the answer, but she didn't know what else to do. Her eyes strafed around the room, looking for something, anything that could help her. She patted her skirt. Where was her phone? Why, after it taking generations of begging, did she *not use her fucking pockets?* Was it still in the bathroom? With no other options, she slid her finger into her mouth, intent on getting whatever it was out of her stomach.

And suddenly, she forgot what she was doing.

The warm, wet sensation of her tongue slipping over her finger was...*wonderful*. Intoxicating. The thick rug tickled her feet, and a fit of giggles bubbled out of her. The pleats of her skirt caressed her ass as she shifted. The breeze of the forced air stroked her bare breasts. She moaned, and the finger in her mouth caressed her tongue.

She didn't notice the smile spreading across Randy's face. At that point, she wouldn't have cared.

27

God damn carpet.

Sam wanted to hear the heavy sound of his feverish pacing, and the carpet was preventing that. You couldn't get a good pace going without the *clomp clomp clomp* of feet hitting the floor. It wasn't just the pacing that he was doing feverishly. He was also checking his phone approximately every three seconds.

Still nothing.

Pace. Look at phone.

Still nothing.

Pace. Look at phone.

Still nothing.

Images careened through his head like the boulder from Indiana Jones, unbidden and unwelcome and definitely about to ruin someone's day. Randy taking Ash's clothes off, kissing up her neck and along her collarbone. Ash slipping down to her knees. Randy bending her over his bed.

Sam wanted to scratch his eyes out. If he thought bashing his head against the wall would drive out the images, he'd do it. He wanted to scream, to throw something against the wall.

Pace. Look at phone.

Still nothing.

Ash shouldn't have to do this!

All he had to do was seal the deal with Veronica. If he hadn't psyched himself out, they wouldn't be in this mess, and Ash wouldn't be losing her virginity before she was ready. Their parents and friends would be fine.

Why did I have to fuck everything up?

He should drive over there and stop her from making the biggest mistake of her life. She laughed at the thought of Randy being her true love. She *knew* Randy wasn't right for her. But then why was she doing it?

Oh, right. Because I fucked up.

He should call Veronica. It might not be too late. If what Ash said was true, then Veronica may still be down to hook up.

If only I wasn't such a bitch. He looked at the clock on his phone. *And if it wasn't already too late for Ash.*

No, he was being too harsh on himself. It wasn't nerves or shyness or embarrassment that stopped him from going all the way with Veronica. It was how he felt about Ash. No...it was *the question* of how he felt about Ash.

Why did he have to overthink everything? Just the thought—just the idea—of having feelings for Ash was enough to stop him from getting with the girl he'd been fantasizing about for years.

Sam shook his head and continued pacing. Preoccupation with his inner demons caused him not to look where he was stepping, and his foot caught on the TV stand. A stack of DVD cases bounced and toppled over, scattering on the floor with a clatter. With an annoyed grunt, he dropped to his knees to clean it up. His eyes caught on an eye-wateringly bright DVD case. It belonged to a cheesy rom-com Ash brought over for them to watch. He stacked it onto the pile of DVDs and put the stack back on the stand, then resumed his pacing. His gaze drifted back to the DVD and Ash's words from the other day came back to him: *Not talking about stuff and keeping secrets are cheap plot devices for teen dramas.*

He almost laughed. Ash assumed he had been asking for advice about what he should do about Veronica, but really he was talking about his fledgling feelings for her. Ash gave him the answer he needed, but he was too chickenshit to act on it then.

This time, the Tercel started on the first try.

You could get to most places in Elsbury in less than ten minutes. Randy's father was rich, however, so they lived on an estate far, far away from where Sam and his mom lived. It should take him thirteen minutes to get there. He did it in eight.

He tried barging through the door, but it was locked, and the thing looked twelve feet tall, so there was no way he was knocking it down. Tamping down his growing frustration, he pounded on the door.

A middle-aged man with salt-and-pepper hair wearing a crisp suit opened it. The man's eyes flitted over Sam and the Tercel, and by the time his gaze got back to Sam, a small sneer rested on his face.

That sneer filled Sam's vision. He was tired of Randy Masters getting what he wanted and getting away with being a douche. He didn't know him, but Sam imagined Randy's dad was the same kind of slimy, smug bastard.

"Yes?"

"I need to see Ash Williams. Is she here?"

The man's eyes didn't move, his face passive and emotionless. "I suggest phoning her if you need to get in touch." He made to close the door, but Sam put his foot in the way.

"It's important. I need to see her."

From somewhere behind the man, Ash's aggravated voice sang out. "Get off me!"

Randy's dad pressed the door against Sam's foot and opened his mouth, no doubt to utter some thinly veiled threat or bullshit excuse, but Sam's fist shut him up.

No time for bullshit.

Sam leapt over the man before he'd settled on the floor. "Ash!" He scanned the foyer, flexing his hand and shaking it. He'd never punched anyone before, and he was unprepared for how much it fucking hurt. A call ricocheted down the hall to the left of the massive staircase that took up most of the foyer.

She sounded scared or maybe hurt.

He careened down the hallway, bouncing off the ornate walls at each turn, following the sound of smooth jazz. The floors, the walls, and even the ceiling were all some fancy, richly textured wood. He felt like the scope in an oak tree's colonoscopy. He rounded the corner into what he'd call the living room. He wasn't sure what it was called in a mansion. Study? Family room? His eyes raked over the room, searching for Ash, and he spotted a pair of shoes behind a large leather couch.

A body.

Leaping over a small table, Sam dropped to his knees beside it.

An evil-looking lump grew from Randy's forehead, a rivulet of blood trickling from it. Shards of glass haloed his head, white with a blue pattern. A dozen feet away there was another explosion of glass. Sam could smell the liquor effervescing into the air. He didn't stop to check Randy's pulse and called out for Ash again.

She could be anywhere. This house is too fucking big.

A sound like a squeak came from near the window, and the drapes rustled like someone was hiding behind them. In his haste to open the curtains, he ripped the rod right off the wall. "Ash!"

"Sam!" She threw herself into his arms, tears streaming down her cheeks and hair in total disarray. She was also completely naked.

Sam shunted aside all the scenarios of why Ash was naked and crying and Randy was concussed on the floor.

"I knew you would come for me."

His arms wrapped around her, and shudders wracked her body. "Why were you hiding in the curtains?"

"I think they're called drapes." Her voice was muffled by his flannel.

"What's the difference?"

Ash sniffled, and when she spoke, her voice came out like she was talking in her sleep. "Rich people have funny names for everything. Cookies aren't cookies. They're biscuits."

"That's *British* people, not rich people."

"Same difference..." Her voice trailed off, and she rubbed her cheek against his flannel, her expression one of rapt pleasure.

"Ash, are you...high?"

"Ugh. Probably." Her cheek didn't stop caressing him. "Shithead over there tried to date rape me."

"Jesus, Ash! Are you okay?"

"I'm fine. He got more than he was expecting..."

"So...does that mean...you didn't...?"

Instead of answering, her hands slid down his back, down and around his hips and back up his chest, to his neck, along his jawline, up past his ears, and through his hair. He started to ask what she was doing, but her fingers slipped into his open mouth. An expression of orgasmic ecstasy overcame her.

He pulled his head. "Blech— What are you d—"

She silenced him with her lips, her tongue sliding across his, and she moaned into his mouth, her whole body shuddering in ecstasy.

Sam was stunned. Both by the sudden change of events and the overwhelming response of his body. He ached to return her kiss, to wrap his arms around her and lay her down on the couch. He pulled away instead.

A small whine slipped from her throat. "Come back. Your lips are so soft..."

He shook his head. "Trust me, I *really* want to."

She grinned, her teeth sharp and white. A low growl came from her throat, and she leaned back in.

"But not like this."

Large green eyes stared into his, so deep and dark he wanted to dive into them. "You always were a pussy."

Then she collapsed in his arms.

28

Ash jerked awake, consciousness suddenly thrust upon her. Her fingernails scratch at the air like she was fending off an attacker. It only took a moment to recognize her own bed. She couldn't remember how she got there. The last thing she recalled was being at Randy's house. The bulge in his robes, the smoky Scotch on his tongue, his body pressed against hers. His hand over her mouth…

Oh fuck.

She looked down at herself, her hands checking her body like she was searching for a knife wound. Under the blankets, she was fully clothed in her favorite pair of pajamas. A relieved sigh was halfway out when the thought struck her.

She had almost been… Randy had almost… Randy *drugged* her!

That fucking bastard!

Images pop into her mind, filling the gaps in her memory. Pushing him away. The chalky pill being forced through her lips. Randy's smug, self-satisfied expression. The shattering vase and the sharp crack it made when she smashed it into his head.

I hope that motherfucker gets brain damage.

It still didn't explain how she got home. Her eyes adjust slowly to the darkness, and her gaze stopped on the beanbag chair where Sam fell asleep. A smile crooked her lips, the memories coming back to her like she was remembering a fleeting dream. Not all the details, but enough that she understood.

Sam came for her. Held her and made sure she was safe. Her face flushed, recalling she had been stark naked, and she had a nagging thought that she'd basically molested him, her hands marveling at the sensation of his jacket over his hard muscles. She'd never given his flannels enough credit. They were *so soft...*

His rough tongue running along her finger. His soft, sweet lips against hers.

Wait a second. *Did I kiss him?*

Maybe being drugged wasn't *all* bad. It gave her the courage to make a move, something she'd been fantasizing about but wouldn't have acted on otherwise. The urge overcame her to stretch like a cat lying in a beam of sunlight. A smile grew on her face, and it didn't show any signs of leaving. Then she remembered Veronica's text.

A pillow hit Sam square in the face.

"Ow!"

A second pillow joined the first.

"Okay, okay. I'm awake!" He peeked out from behind the pillow he held up for protection. "Oh, thank god, you're awake. Are you—"

Ash threw a third pillow, which Sam easily deflected. "You asshole!" She looked around for something else to throw.

"What? What did I do?"

"*What did you do?* You tell me, you fucking liar."

THE ACCURSED

"Nothing happened, I swear! I brought you home, got you dressed, and put you in bed. That's it!"

"Aren't you a knight in shining fucking armor? You didn't take advantage of a drugged girl. Congratufuckinglations!"

"I get the feeling you're not happy about something."

"I'm talking about you and Veronica!"

"What are you—"

"You said nothing happened, but I got a text from her that had *a lot* more to say."

"Oh."

"Oh? OH? That's all you have to say!?"

Sam struggled up from the beanbag, raising his hands to surrender or calm her it didn't matter She wasn't having it. "I don't know what she told you, but I can explain."

"Explain?" Her voice rose an octave, and she whipped the covers off her with a snap. "Explain how you got a blowjob but couldn't sack up enough to seal the deal? How you were going to let our parents die? You can explain? Explain how you were going to let me have sex with Randy even though you knew I wasn't ready? Explain that!" She leapt out of bed intending to jab her finger into his chest, but her legs weren't ready to support her. She stumbled and would have fallen if Sam hadn't caught her.

"I've got you." His voice was soft and quiet.

Ash took a deep breath and exhaled some of her pent-up anger. She nodded, her cheek brushing against his T-shirt. "I know."

He helped her back to the bed and sat next to her. "You're right. I lied about Veronica." He rubbed his face like he was trying to scrub away bad memories. "Things weren't going well at the restaurant, and she was flirting with the waiter. I thought I blew it. She said the date was a bust, but as I made a fool of myself trying to salvage things, she suggested we get a hotel room." He blew out his lips and ran a hand through his hair. "Things were *definitely* heading in the right direction at the hotel."

Ash's stomach tightened, but she stayed silent.

"She gave me a... She started to..."

"Blow you. Jesus, Sam. Grow a pair already."

"Fine! She started to blow me. Happy? But I..." His voice trailed off, and he shook his head. "I couldn't stop thinking about you."

"Eww!"

"Not like that. I mean I couldn't go through with it. I stopped her, and I got out of there."

"Really?"

Sam smiled, the worry lines easing from around his eyes a bit, and he almost looked boyish. "Yeah, right? I should get a medal or something. The first guy to stop mid-blowjob."

She punched him in the shoulder. "Why didn't you just tell me?"

Sam let out a deep breath. "Because—"

"Because you're a pussy," she finished for him.

He nodded. "Yes, that. But things were complicated. I've..." He trailed off again, then seemed to muster some courage and forged ahead in a rush. "I realized a few days ago that I still have feelings for you. But I didn't know how to tell you. Because you were with Randy, and I didn't want to get between you."

Despite the warm fire kindling in her stomach, a question fluttered around her brain. "Still?"

A blush crawled up his neck and blazed across his face. "Um...yeah... I've sorta liked you since the eighth grade."

"Why didn't you ever say anything?"

"Because I was a shy kid. Because I didn't know how. Because we were best friends, and after losing our parents..."

He didn't have to finish the sentence. "You didn't want to risk losing me, too." She knew that fear all too well.

They lapsed into silence, neither one saying anything or daring to look the other in the eye.

"Why did you show up at Randy's house?"

"I couldn't stop thinking about what you said. About not keeping secrets and how people should tell each other how they feel. So, I came to tell you before it was too late."

"Did you beat the door down?" She nodded to his knuckles, which were red and scraped raw.

"Oh, um..." He laughed nervously and dragged his hand through his hair again. "I sorta...knocked Randy's dad out."

"You *what*?"

He told her about trying to barge into Randy's house, how his dad answered, and how he wouldn't let Sam in to talk to Ash. Then, with no little embarrassment, he told her that he punched the man in the face and jumped over him to find her. By the time he was done, her hands covered her mouth.

"Oh my god, Sam."

"I know..."

"*No*, Sam. Oh my god... You didn't!"

He finally caught on that he was missing something. "What? What is it?"

"That wasn't Randy's dad."

"WHAT?"

"That was the butler!" Ash broke into uncontrolled laughter. "Randy's dad…is still…in Atlantic City."

"Please tell me you're joking." Laughter stopped her from answering, tears streaming down her cheeks. "It's not *that* funny! I just assaulted a guy."

"Eh, he's only a butler."

"That's a little harsh."

"He was protecting a date rapist, Sam"

"…But fair." Sam nodded, clearly feeling better about his class A misdemeanor.

She bumped his shoulder. "It was very gallant. I appreciate you knocking out the hired help to save me."

Sam's hand tentatively reached over and grabbed hers. "When I got there, Randy was unconscious, and you were…naked." His voice dropped to a whisper like he was afraid to ask. "What happened?"

Ash wished then she hadn't thrown all the pillows. She needed something to hide behind. She had never been good at *feelings*. Emoting wasn't really her thing. But, she supposed, Sam mustered the courage to tell her how he felt, so she could at least do the same.

She told him what happened. How she threw herself at Randy and—with a deep breath, she rushed through this next part—how she realized Randy wasn't the one she really wanted to be with. Told him how she had to escape to the bathroom because she was almost a gibbering mess. How she'd just decided to not go through with it when she received Veronica's text. Sam winced when she explained how the text fueled her decision to have sex with Randy.

THE ACCURSED

Then she told him that she couldn't go through with it and how Randy had given her a party drug to get her in the mood.

"That asshole!"

"Don't worry, I took care of them."

Sam chuckled darkly. "Yeah, no kidding. I saw." They were silent for a moment until he finally spoke. "So... Veronica's text made you mad?"

Their eyes met, and a knowing grin appeared on his lips. She rolled her eyes and stayed silent until he persisted with a raised eyebrow. "Fine! Yes, all right? I was jealous. Happy? Even though our families are in trouble, I admit I was happy when I thought nothing happened between the two of you."

"So why didn't you tell me?"

A beat of silence passed, and they answered at the same time.

"Because I'm a pussy."

"Because you're a pussy."

They burst into laughter.

She wiped the tears of mirth from her eyes. "So...what now?"

Sam glanced toward the window where the sky was turning from red-orange to purple. "We've got about an hour until the new moon..."

She hit him again. "Are you really trying to get in my pants? *Now*?"

Sam held up his hands in surrender. "Only to save the world!"

She burst into laughter. "God, I don't know if that's the worst or the best pickup line I've ever heard."

"Depends if it works or not."

Ash grinned and leaned against him, brushing her lips against his.

"I guess we'll just have to see..."

29

A WEEK AGO, IF someone asked her if she was ready to lose her virginity, she would have laughed and said no. She wasn't a prude. She did other stuff. Plenty of stuff, in fact. She didn't begrudge girls like Veronica who took charge of their sexuality. They knew what they were doing and made their own choices, just as she made hers. Ash was a wild kid, she knew that about herself, but she also knew she wasn't ready to make *that* particular leap.

Until that night, apparently. Until Sam.

It wasn't like it would have been with Randy. It wasn't *just* about breaking the curse.

Okay, the whole coma thing provided *a little* urgency to the situation, but even without the curse, she was confident she and Sam would have been popping each other's cherries sooner or later. It just so happened that it was sooner.

Ash wasn't sure if the drugs still lingered in her system or if Sam's touch was just that arousing. If she didn't know better, she'd think he'd had practice. But that wasn't the case. They told each other everything, there was no way she wouldn't know. Also, he did enough fumbling and apologizing that there was no way he'd done any of it before.

"Is that too hard?" He sucked on her left nipple and ran his rough tongue over it.

The only response Ash could give was a deep moan. She hadn't known she liked her breasts played with. Randy had access to them many times, but—typical guy—he always had his sights below the belt and spent little time above.

Too bad, she decided when she could finally formulate a coherent thought between waves of pleasure. *If he had, he might have gotten what he so desperately wanted.* It was good Randy hadn't. She didn't want to share this moment with anyone but Sam.

The scene beyond the open curtains was like a ticking clock, a countdown to zero hour when their lives would change forever. She couldn't shake the feeling they were being watched. There was a cloud of anticipation in the air like it wasn't just her and Sam in the room, like the whole town had been waiting for this moment. In a way, she guessed it had been.

For years people had been telling them she and Sam made a good couple. She chalked the feeling up to nerves and pushed the worry away. Sam's wet, rough tongue slid across her nipple again, and she bit her lip to keep from crying out.

"Jesus, Sam," she gasped, "you've been holding out on me."

His mouth broke free of her skin with a wet pop. "I was on the debate team freshman and sophomore years. I've always been good with my tongue." He demonstrated with another caress of her nipple. "You could even call me a *master* debater."

She groaned and put her hands on his head. "Less puns, more tongue." She pushed his head down her body.

"Yes, ma'am." He answered between kisses, working his way down her sternum, over her stomach...and kept going.

"Oh! Oh, yeah. Yep, more of that. Lots more of that." Her toes curled. Five of the most euphoric minutes of her life later, she experienced her first orgasm with another person. Randy had *technically* been there for one before, but she had done most of the work.

Now, it's my turn. A grin stretched her lips, and she wasn't sure who was more excited, her or Sam.

He didn't seem to mind that she couldn't take all of him in her mouth. She gagged going to the dentist, so there was no way she'd be able to deepthroat him. Ash never spent much time pondering blowjob technique. For example, what should she do with her hands? It wasn't something she had to worry about with Randy since there was no need to get her hands involved. Sam was a different story, so she learned as she went.

He didn't seem disappointed with her technique a few minutes later when she was spitting out the result of her efforts.

"Wow. That was...amazing." He wrapped his arm around her, pulling her close.

Wiping her mouth on her discarded shirt, she leaned in and gave him a kiss. "You realize you'll have to give up your medal for stopping mid-blowjob."

"Worth it." He kissed her again.

After they broke apart from the kiss, she snuggled into his chest. "I don't think this is what the painting meant when it said 'cleave.'"

She could hear the grin in his voice. "Give me a few minutes, and we'll see what we can do about that."

"Just a few minutes?" Sam nodded. "What ever will we do until then?"

"I can think of a few things..." His strong hands grabbed her thighs, and he flipped her onto her back.

It took longer than a few minutes for them to get to the cleaving. Sam was ready in a few like he said, but she wouldn't let him move on until he finished what he started.

They slowed down after that. Not just because the enormity of what was at stake was hovering over them, but because Sam kept stopping to check that she was comfortable.

"Everything okay?" he asked her over and over, followed by, "are you sure?"

It was very sweet, but by the third repetition of the questions, she wanted to grab him by the balls and tell him to give it to her already. So that was exactly what she did.

It turned out, all the fashion magazines were right. Communication during sex was key.

Not wearing a condom went against everything their parents and teachers taught them, but the last thing they wanted was to violate the unspoken terms of the blessing because of a technicality.

It could still be the drugs, but she reveled in the sensation of Sam inside her. At first, their motions were awkward, inexperienced. Once the feeling that the world was about to end was shunted aside, their bodies began to move in harmony with each other. The awkwardness of inexperience gave way, and a sense of urgency overtook them, not driven by foreboding doom but by their biological need to be with each other.

After he got his sea legs under him, Sam paid more attention to her breasts without disrupting his rhythm. *Yep, I'm definitely a boob gal.*

Ash reached down and gave Sam's dangly fellas a squeeze. She was rewarded by a loud moan, the reverberation of it vibrating her breast, and she was sure he was about to pop. It was enough to send her over the edge, and ecstasy flowed through her. He slowed but didn't stop, his gaze finding hers, looking at her with such tenderness she nearly melted.

"You didn't come?"

He shook his head. "Nah, I pre-gamed a few times while you slept. I can go for a while longer."

"*Pre-gamed*? Samael Phillips Dyer did you *expect* to get lucky tonight?" She laughed, not knowing whether she should be impressed or shocked at his presumption.

In response, he leaned down and kissed her neck, then slid himself completely inside her. She gasped, and a post-orgasm shiver coursed through her body.

"Disappointed?" he asked, no little amount of teasing in his voice.

Biting her lip, all she could do was shake her head. "Sam Dyer…" She couldn't continue until she caught her breath. "You were much less cocky before I popped your cherry."

"That's funny. I could say the same thing about you."

She groaned at the pun. "Shut up and get back to work."

"Yes, ma'am." A sheepish grin crept onto his face. "Do you…wanna try it from behind?"

The answer, it turned out, was *yes*. Over the next twenty minutes, she said—and screamed—that same word many times. The second—or was it third?—time Sam took her from behind, her hands clutched the cold steel rods of her bed's footboard. Her gaze fell on the painting hanging on the wall.

The two lovers depicted embraced each other, bodies intertwined like the twisting branches of the tree above them. She almost shook her head that she ever thought that she and Randy could be like them. Randy was always down to fuck, but she doubted he had the capacity to hold someone so tenderly as the man in the painting.

Ash threw Sam onto his back and straddled him, her eyes still on the painting as she began to grind and rock her hips. The position left Sam's hands free to explore her body, and explore they did. One hand found her right breast, and the other slipped down to rub between her legs. A hot urge built inside her.

Sam's mouth opened in a moan, his hands' work forgotten. Ash fought it, pushing the climax back as long as she could, building up the crescendo. Her nails dug into his chest, and he stiffened inside her. Sam's hands wrapped around her hips, and he ground himself into her.

The ecstasy built and built. He filled her so fully it was almost painful. They couldn't hold back the cresting wave any longer.

30

Their bodies convulsed, and their mouths opened to shout in ecstasy. But the sound that ripped through her throat wasn't a cry of passion.

It was pain. Blinding, agonizing pain.

The room disappeared from her vision. Pain blinded her to everything except the fire running along her nerves. Sam's fingers dug into her flesh, and she knew he was experiencing it, too.

Why does it feel like this?

She'd heard your first time could hurt, but she didn't expect anything like this. This wasn't her first orgasm. It wasn't even the first time something had been inside her. Was it the drugs Randy gave her? *Am I still tripping?*

But pain wracked her, and her mind couldn't follow that train of thought. She lost track of time, lost track of everything. When the shroud of pain finally lifted and her consciousness came screaming back to her, she didn't know how long it had been.

Her body ached like she'd completed the hardest workout of her life. Like she'd had the shit kicked out of her. The wave of anguish was gone for only a few moments until a new realization slammed into her. She couldn't move.

Her body was stuck like she'd been cast in iron, a statue made of flesh. Only her eyes could roll in their sockets. Beneath her, Sam was as still as a stone. Still hard as he was minutes ago and still in her. Moments ago, having him inside her filled her with unbridled ecstasy, but now it was just...wrong. She felt violated.

What felt good just a few moments ago was now a foreign and unwelcome sensation. It was the Randy situation all over again. A man forcing his will upon her without her consent. She wanted to scream, to push herself off him. She wanted to lash out and hit him. But it wasn't Sam's fault. He was as confused and terrified as she was. She couldn't see much, but she could see the confusion and pain in his eyes.

A movement caught her eye. A dim orange glow from the streetlamps filtered through the parted curtains. Across the room, there was another source of light. The painting. It was glowing. Some trick of the orange light made it look like the branches squirmed within the frame. Writhing like snakes.

But it wasn't a trick of the light. The branches and roots were moving, filling the room with scritching-scratching sounds. Sam's eyes rolled in their sockets, desperate to understand and searching for the source of the sound. He was terrified. She knew because she was, too.

Her eyes fixed on the couple in the painting. A few short days ago, even a few moments earlier, she had marveled at their loving embrace. She daydreamed about one day finding someone to hold her like that. Ash realized now how wrong she was. It wasn't ecstasy or love or adoration. It was terror. Abject terror. They didn't cling to each other in a lover's embrace, their bodies writhing together in lovemaking. Like cavemen huddling together during a winter storm, the couple gripped each other in fear. Fear of what was out there.

Fear of what's coming.

Ash's eyes boggled when the wriggling vines burst forth from the painting. They splayed and spread across the wall like somebody dropped a bottle of ink.

A sharp pain lanced her thigh, and she cried out. She couldn't move her tongue or her jaw, but her mouth was wide open, frozen during her exultant cry of passion. She could still scream.

Sam searched for the source of her pain, but he still couldn't move his head. He found out soon enough why she screamed. Something dark and thin snaked out of the bed and along Sam's neck. *It's a root*, she realized. It wriggled up to Sam's face, and without preamble, burrowed itself through his cheek. His eyes widened in pain, and he joined her in voicing his agony.

Ash screamed again. Not in pain, but in anger and frustration. And because she could feel dozens of the roots squirming along her body. Minutes ago, she and Sam were doing their own writhing, their hands and mouths exploring each other's bodies in a way they'd only dreamed before. Eagerness and desire had chased away any trepidation she had about losing her virginity.

Now, the only thing they shared was pain and horror.

The roots crisscrossed their bodies like they'd been captured by a giant spider. Even if some unseen force wasn't holding them motionless, she doubted they'd be able to break free from the prison. The vines were abrasive, and they scratched her skin raw. The scent of blood quickly overtook the smell of sweat and sex.

A root circled the girth of Sam's penis, the thing tickling the hair between her legs. She tried to shy away from it, but she still couldn't move. Sweat sheened Sam's body, and he struggled to break free from whatever force held them. The bed shivered with his effort, but it was no use. His eyes widened, and then he made a sound she'd never heard before, the shriek tearing through his throat and shredding vocal cords into ground meat.

Sam's still-erect penis shivered and jerked inside of her. Confusion flitted through her brain. Why was he screaming like someone had doused him in gasoline and set him on fire?

The confusion was propelled out of her a moment later when the worst pain she'd ever experienced lanced through her.

A tendril had pierced Sam's penis. It feasted on the bloody contents of his corpus cavernosum and used those nutrients to continue its growth, growing ever upward toward its next feast. It squirmed upward, bulging out of Sam's glans like a pustule. Then it burst forth and burrowed into her vaginal wall.

The scream ripped out of her chest and tore her vocal cords to shreds.

31

The bloodroots stopped pulsing. Some had absorbed enough energy they were as thick as a forearm. So many roots covered the room, only slivers of what lay beneath peeked through. Canary yellow latex paint, posters featuring angry women wielding guitars, pictures of the girl with her father, with her lover, with other friends.

The wall that held the painting was so thick with vines and roots that it looked like a solid wall of wood. The only splash of color on the wall was a small rectangular picture of the huddling, frightened couple.

Beside the painting, among the woven roots, a darker rectangle appeared like a hole in the darkest pits of Hell.

A shoe stepped through the hole, the end of a foreleg attached to it. It hovered in the air like its owner was simply stepping from the garden path to the stoop rather than from across the vast emptiness of space and time itself.

The dark brown Oxford loafer lowered and came to rest on the floor. Presently, the rest of the gentleman followed. He looked like a man stepped out of time. Well-dressed in a fitted sack suit, matching trousers, and contrasting vest. A long black cane and a bowler hat completed the ensemble. He was young, not much older than Sam, but his eyes had seen the passing of eons.

The young gentleman looked down as if seeing himself for the first time. He brushed the sleeves of his suit with a tender caress and gave his cane a jaunty tap on the floor. He took in the room for the first time, and the pencil mustache adorning his lip twitching in disappointment.

"That won't do at all." He spoke in a rich, lightly accented proper Queen's English. The cane tapped again, and a crisp, white light illuminated the room. Nodding, satisfied, he noticed the motionless forms of the two erstwhile lovers, his thin mustache twitched in irritation.

Though a thick pink rug padded the floor, his hard-heeled shoes clacked as if he strode through an ancient stone dungeon, for no reason other than that was the way a man's shoes *should* sound. Approaching the bed, he leaned over until his face was inches away from the girl's, like he was inspecting a curious and well-made taxidermy. A noncommittal grunt was the only sound he made.

The two young humans resembled root-bound trees, the blood-seeking vines piercing their bodies every which way. Despite being riddled with holes, pierced by dozens of vines, the skin around each wound didn't weep. The vines were too greedy to allow such wastefulness.

The movement was so subtle the dapper gentleman wouldn't have seen it if he were human: the nape of their necks jerked with minute flutters. The twitching shudder of a weak pulse.

"Hmm." The spell hadn't worked. *Not entirely, at least.*

THE ACCURSED

He looked down at his body again, inspecting his hands like he expected them to pop off and run away at any second. With a pensive expression, he turned toward the room at large, his eyes alighting on a short table at the end of the bed. Hitching his cane under his arm and a hand on his bowler, he ran full tilt at the table. The young gentleman crashed into it and sprawled to the floor, his hat pitching from his head in the tumult. Springing to his feet, he laughed gaily.

The summoning worked!

It didn't just work, it worked better than he could have hoped. His eyes darted from side to side as he pondered the reasons, and his gaze stopped on the shuddering forms of the lovers.

"Ah, young love." He approached the bed again, and he saw that the commotion had brought the two to fragile consciousness.

"That explains why you're still alive." He laughed again, spinning his cane like a baton twirler. Two sets of eyes watched him. They couldn't speak, but he imagined he knew the question on their minds.

"The spell wasn't designed to bring me over. Not *all the way over*, you understand. It should have taken months, perhaps years, for me to gather enough strength to become corporeal. But you two..." He booped the pair on their noses.

"Young love," he said again, as if that explained everything. Pursing his lips, he looked at them through squinted eyes. "*True* love," he corrected. He circled the bed to the other side, the pair's silent eyes following him as best they could. He leaned down again, inspecting the pair from a new angle.

A spicy scent like that of ants snaked its way up Sam's and Ash's nostrils.

"I see you are confounded. How you lot escaped the caves astounds me to no end. Very well, I'll endeavor to explain in terms you'll understand.

"Any sort of coitus would have sufficed for the original...*spell*." He spat the last like it was an unpalatable flavor. "It's a pedestrian charm, really, and its call for true love is...an affectation. Love, like all human emotions—lust, for example—is power. Without my interference, the power would have fueled the original blessing."

The man smiled and danced a jaunty, straight-backed little jig, his shoes clacking against the floor. After another tap of his cane, his voice dropped like he was sharing a secret with two confidantes. "It was rather clever supplanting that swamp witch's blessing for my summoning. The way you humans rut with each other, I thought it would be no time at all before my return. Alas, the painting fell into the hands of that spinster, where it languished for decades. And then when she finally succumbed, it passed on to those wretched sodomites. Practically monks, those two."

His eyes flicked to Sam as if the boy had said something. "To think, tying my fate to a love charm that spent seventy years in the hands of the willfully celibate. Humans are...unpredictable." He flourished his hands in the air with a shrug.

The man—if he could be called a man—pulled out an ornate silver watch from his vest pocket, tutted, and snapped it closed. "Deepest apologies, children, but I've places to be. I had hoped to be further along in my plans, especially when you, young miss"—he indicated Ash—"acquired the painting. Alas, it seems the youth of today are not as puissant as they once were."

THE ACCURSED

He tipped his hat to them and turned to leave. A sound like a man taking his last breath stopped him. He turned and walked back, his face so close they could see that his skin was smooth and free of pores. His pupils were vertical slits like a predator's.

Those terrifying eyes locked onto Sam. "Did you say something?" His tone was intense, more curious than threatening.

Another noise sounded in Sam's throat, and the man laughed. "Like I said, unpredictable! How marvelous! Now, boy, what are you trying to say?"

"W..." Sam's words came out like he hadn't had water for weeks, the root growing through his cheeks muffling the sound further. "Wh-hhhy..."

The man pursed his lips. "Why?" He repeated it like he didn't understand the word. "Why, why, why, why..." His hand went to his breast pocket where he'd tucked the pocket watch away. "I suppose you want to know why all this"—he waved his hand to encompass the room—"happened." He waited for Sam to respond, but nothing more came.

The gentleman looked disappointed. "There are so many mysteries. So many wonders. To waste an opportunity and ask for a *reason*...but very well.

"Why am I here? That, I won't answer. Why you...why *this*... Well, because I needed the power. Why all the deaths surrounding you?" A cruel smile grew on his face, inhumanly wide like a frog's. "Because of *you two*. If you had simply fornicated, no one else need suffer. That first day, when you initiated the charm, my summoning would have drained you dry. But your parents and friends would have been safe. For a while, at least.

"Oh, but how you fought!" He threw his head back and cackled. "You let morality guide you rather than your bestial urges." He shook his head, disgusted or impressed they didn't know. "The other deaths were...incentive. The summoning needed to be finished. I required just one of you to rut like the savages you are. When it appeared you wouldn't succumb on your own, I took matters into my own hands. Inflaming your and others' desires to better ensnare you. *That* was a costly intervention. One I was loathe to employ, but you children were just so obstinate."

Their eyes widened, each rocked by his words and thinking the same thing. *Scotty. Mr. Pinkett. Mrs. Murray. Veronica.*

The man's hand came up and caressed Sam's cheek. "Nevertheless, you denied me. Denied yourselves." His lip curled into a snarl, and he grabbed Sam's jaw with two fingers. A whine slipped out of Sam, and something in his mouth shifted with a wet, muffled pop. A rivulet of blood trickled from the corner of his mouth.

The man's gaze dropped to the hand holding Sam, like he'd noticed it for the first time. He released him, flexing and splaying his fingers, marveling at something the two humans couldn't fathom. "But I suppose in the end, I should thank you. Though you meandered and dawdled, your coupling was...unpredictable." He shook his head and laughed wryly. "Love. It provided power a magnitude above what copulation would have. It not only opened the doorway, but it gave me form. I suppose I owe you thanks for that. Perhaps I'm ahead of schedule after all."

His dark eyes considered the motionless pair, the silvered pommel of his cane tapping against his lips as he thought. The hardwood cane rapped against the floor once, twice, thrice. On the third, whatever invisible force held them released. Their bodies slumped against the roots piercing them, igniting fresh, burning agony. Now that they had full control of their mouths and throats, they screamed.

"Ah, yes. Apologies."

Two more taps of his cane and the roots shriveled. Within seconds, the tendrils looked like desiccated umbilical cords. An expression almost like sadness filled the gentleman's eyes as the roots crumbled to dust.

The two broken and bleeding bodies collapsed onto the bed, silent but for the whimpering and hushed sobs. So slow it could be measured in geologic time, Sam and Ash inched toward each other. Even through the crippling haze of pain, seeking each other's embrace.

At the wretched sight, the gentleman's lip curled in disgust. The delicious, heady scent of agony intermingled with the grotesque aroma of tears, sweat, and musk of sex. His stomach churned with hunger even while his gorge rose. He had to turn away from the sight before he vomited. The thought of such a base, human act sent his stomach roiling more and hot anger shot through him. With clenched teeth, he clamped down on his nausea. His voice was shaky with suppressed sick.

"Though you did it in ignorance, you did me a service. I suppose I owe you a debt. The least I can do is offer a quick death." Swallowing the bile in his throat, he turned, fortifying himself for the wretched sight.

Their bodies were so covered in blood and bruises, it was hard to discern them from each other. Arms wrapped around each other, Ash's face pressed firmly against Sam's chest. Tears streamed down their cheeks, intermingling with the dried blood. Sam stroked Ash's hair, his lips moved, but even with the gentleman's preternatural hearing he couldn't make out the words. Discounting the blood, tears, and open wounds, the tableau was a close reproduction of the painting on the wall. The painting that had acted as both the door to his prison and the window through which he observed this plane of existence.

A sensation like fire ants burrowing into their skin blazed across Ash and Sam's bodies. They cried out and held each other tighter. The sensation didn't recede as it would if they slipped into unconsciousness and death. Instead, the pain intensified. Hesitantly, they opened their eyes, first looking at each other before turning to the wounds across their bodies. As they watched, the holes that pocked their skin began to close. A dull, wet *click* came from Sam's mouth, and he felt his broken teeth slip back into place. Within moments, their wounds were gone, replaced by angry, red welts.

The gentleman took a deep breath, and though his body didn't so much as move, he seemed to shrink. Like he suddenly took up less space in the world. He opened his eyes, an indiscernible expression on his face. "That is as much as you'll get from me."

For the first time since this had all began, Sam realized they were still naked. He pulled Ash into his arms to shield her from the stranger's penetrating gaze. They huddled against each other, weeping. Sam spat out a mouthful of blood.

The man's heels clacked toward the bedroom door. Before he disappeared through the portal, he turned back. "I trust you'll keep this just between us?" He twirled a finger in the air to indicate everything that had transpired. It was phrased as a question, but the two knew it for what it was: a threat.

"I'd hate to take more from you than I already have. Live your remaining lives well, Ashley and Samael." He bent into a shallow bow and tipped his hat. "I thank you again for your sacrifice and hospitality.

"Hail, Ygg-hatep." And with that, he was gone.

Epilogue

It took three weeks for Sam and Ash to leave her house. Three weeks avoiding the outside world, of coming to terms with their scars, physical and emotional. The gentleman took more from them than just their blood. The wounds in their flesh healed, leaving a handful of scars the size of pinpricks.

But that wasn't the worst.

When they finally woke two days later, it was only to discover that everyone who had been in a coma was still unconscious.

The doctors called it a pandemic. They didn't know what caused it, but calling it a pandemic allowed them to fit the deaths into a nice little box that they didn't have to think much about.

Judy. Three of their classmates. Four of their teachers.

Their parents.

They were stable but unresponsive. The doctors weren't optimistic about a recovery and gave Sam and Ash information about end-of-life options. They'd lost so much they couldn't make those decisions yet.

Luckily, MU Sanitarium, the research hospital over in Arkham, offered to take in all the patients, the researchers there confident about a positive outcome. Sam and Ash agreed to the offer, relieved they didn't have to consider the alternative and for MU's generous grants and discounts for local patients.

All they had left was each other. It would have been easy after everything had happened to run away from each other, to run away from intimacy and love, but on the third night after they woke, Ash went to the guest bedroom where Sam slept. Ash had taken up in her dad's room, not able to return to her own.

She slipped into the bed without a word. She didn't have to say anything. They lived through something horrific together, losing everyone important to them and a part of themselves in the process. They took solace in each other's company. They wouldn't let the mysterious gentleman take that from them, too. Most nights they just held each other and talked. Sometimes laughing, sometimes crying, but always in each other's arms.

They still ached from their wounds. Whatever the gentleman had done to them had only accelerated their healing, so when they finally did make love, their motions were slow and gentle, more hesitant than they were even that first night. Afterwards, they lay in each other's arms and wept.

At some point, the bed in the guest room stopped being Sam's and became theirs. A few weeks later, they packed Ash's clothes and those mementos she couldn't bear to leave and moved into his mom's house—now, his house. Though their parents were still alive, the court gave them control of their parents' assets. They weren't sure if they'd keep Ash's house or sell it, but she wasn't ready to make that decision.

On their last night in the Williams' house, Sam pulled down the ladder that led to the small attic. Ash's room took up most of the top floor, so the attic was more of a broom closet, filled with holiday decorations and some of her mom's old stuff that somehow survived the purge. He opened an old box, dislodging seven years' worth of dust. He had to remove some old photo albums and what looked like a wedding dress, yellowed with age like a hunk of old ivory, in order to fit the painting in the box.

Like the house itself, they weren't sure what to do with the painting. They talked about it but couldn't decide between researching its history or destroying it. One thing was for sure: they weren't going to pass it on to anyone else. Whatever they did in the interim, they vowed they'd be the curse's final victims.

The stairs rattled and ascended back into the ceiling. Sam dusted himself off and returned to helping Ash pack up her things.

They weren't ready to talk about the painting or what happened with the mysterious gentleman. The last they said on the matter was to agree not to tell anyone what really happened that night. No one would believe them, anyway.

They moved across town into Sam's house and began putting their lives back together. Senior year was almost over. After that…who knew what else. College? Careers? Marriage? The future held too many uncertainties, and for now, they were focused on healing.

It was hard to think about the future when they knew something dark was out there. Something powerful. Something with vertical eyes. Something evil.

Whatever it was, they had unleashed it.

But they weren't ready to talk about that.

RIAIN FOX

The world was a new and dazzling place. It was livelier and bursting with energy. Cars. Aeroplanes. He could feel the hum of power running along the black lines overhead.

Electricity. That was the word. The primates had it the last time he was on this plane, but there was so much more now. *Excess.* That's what he saw as he stood on the girl's porch. This age was fueled by excess. No matter. It was a bounteous harvest that awaited his reaping.

A motorcar passed, spewing both noxious fumes and a clamorous racket. Once it passed, he could hear their incessant weeping coming from the girl and her lover. He could taste the saltiness of the blood and tears that covered their naked bodies.

A pleasant stirring kindled in his gut. It was equal parts titillating and loathsome.

The disadvantages of being confined to the human form.

For a moment, the sensation overwhelmed even the stifling presence of his master. He experienced his master's incessant ire with a sense beyond that which his fragile human suit could fathom. It was more than feel, more than touch or taste. It beat against his very being from across the unfathomable cosmos. Driving him forward to his glorious purpose.

The breeze wafted through the abode, bringing with it another briny scent redolent with pain and lust and terror. His internal organs grumbled again.

Perhaps there is time for one meal...

Lanterns from a motorcar drifted across the grass and something caught his eye. Beside the boy's own motorcar, he bent and picked up a rumpled pile of cloth. The vulgar chemise the girl wore to seduce her erstwhile paramour, forgotten where it fell when the boy carried her into the home.

The gentleman's gaze turned to the east, toward the homes that housed this village's gentry. His lips lifted, the rictus resembling something like a smile.

Yes, perhaps there's time for one meal.

THE END

If you'd like to see what happens when the gentleman joins Randy and his father for a meal, download the exclusive bonus chapters here: readerlinks.com/l/354833

Thank you for reading *The Accursed*, book 1 of Eldritch Affair. I hope you enjoyed it and are eager to get your hands on book 2, *The Herald*. Pick it up from your favorite online bookstore today at books2read.com/the-herald

To keep up to date with what I'm up to and newest releases, please join my mailing list at ryanwfox.com/nlsu-riain/

Books these days succeed or fail based on the strength of their reviews. I hope you will consider leaving a review with your favorite retailer or at Goodreads: goodreads.com/review/new/194281276

Thank you for reading!

Bloopers

THE SCENT OF COCONUT and chlorine wafted with each stroke of Mrs. Murray's hand. Warm, supple breasts pressed against Sam's chest but he had a hard time focusing on anything other than what Mrs. Murray's hands were doing.

"Um...HELLO?" Mike Murray's voice was hesitant, aggravated. The sound of it finally caught Sam's attention. Mike's brow was wrinkled, consternation clearly evident on his face. "I said: 'Mom, what the hell?' That's your cue to stop and turn to me in surprise."

It took a moment for the words to process, then comprehension dawned. Sam looked down to Mrs. Murray, but it appeared she hadn't even noticed her son appearing. The rhythmic pumping of her hand never missed a beat.

"Um, Mrs. Murray?" Sam had to repeat himself two times before she glanced up. "Mike's here..." Sam jerked his head toward the younger man. She glanced over, but didn't let it stop her efforts.

Mike, for his part, looked extremely uncomfortable. "Mom, you're supposed to stop," he said in the tone of a young teen imploring his mom not to embarrass him in front of his friends.

"I can't, sweetie," she said, turning back to Sam.

"What? Why?"

"Do you know how long it's been since I've had a good fuck?"

"I thought you and Mr. Murray had an open relationship."

"What!? Ew, Mom. Gross!"

"Oh, grow up, honey. Now run off and do your homework. Momma's gonna see if she can still deepthroat." The water splashed he she dropped to her knees. "Lord knows I haven't been able to practice on your father."

"Mom!"

"I know. Genetics are a bitch. But you're a good boy and not bad looking. You'll do fine. Now, run off before your future therapist bill becomes astronomical. I don't think you'll want to see this..."

SAM'S ABDOMEN AND FACE hurt from all the laughing. He wouldn't be surprised if he was sporting welts where Ash's fingers dug into his ribs.

But that was the last thing on his mind right then. The taste of her lips lingered on his and he could feel the rush of blood to his face just as his heart was speeding up. Ash had an impish grin and she shifted her weight to jump off him. Before she could, Sam caught her wrist. Her eyes widened, expecting retribution in the way of tickling, or maybe a pillow to the head, but her expression turned to confusion when she saw the earnest look on his face.

"What's up, Sam?"

He was quiet for a long moment. Thoughts and feelings he thought long-buried flitted through his mind. Finally, just as Ash was starting to worry about his mental state, Sam spoke, and the words nearly bowled her over.

"I love you."

A giggle was halfway up her throat when everything clicked together. The earnest expression, the somber tone. Tears fuzzed her vision and she dropped back down on top of him and planted another kiss on his lips. This time, a real one. "I love you too."

Neither of them could say how long they sat there, exploring each others' mouths and tongues with their own. Finally, after what seemed like hours and yet somehow only seconds, they parted with a gasp.

"So now what?" Sam asked, looking up at his best friend. Her face was flushed and her chest heaved, pulling her shirt tight against her body.

The impish grin returned and she pressed her body against his. "I'm guessing this isn't a zucchini you're hiding in your pants?" Sam flushed, embarrassed that she'd noticed his obvious arousal. She laughed, a deep and guttural chuckle. "It's okay, Sam. Really."

Their eyes met and a silence blossomed between them, a pregnant, heavy silence that grew and grew until a small, happy smile pulled at Ash's lips and Sam finally asked.

"So...do you...wanna have sex?"

The End

BESIDE THE PAINTING, AMONG the woven roots, a darker rectangle appeared like a hole in the darkest pits of Hell.

A shoe stepped through the dark rectangle, the end of a foreleg attached to it. It hovered in the air like its owner was simply stepping from the garden path to the stoop rather than from across the vast emptiness of space and time itself.

The dark brown Oxford loafer lowered and came to rest on the floor...and slipped.

A well-dressed gentleman with a cane and a bowler hat tumbled out of the interdimensional portal and landed, sprawled, on the root-strewn floor.

The young man of indeterminate age popped up from the floor, his bowler askew over his eyes. He clutched the cane with both hands like it was a lifeline and his legs shook like he'd had a night at the pub with the boys. His whole body shook as he steadied himself. Finally, when the trembling was mostly under control, he lifted a tentative hand and straightened his hat.

"Sorry," he said in a voice that sounded much like a young John Cleese. "It's been ages since I've had corporeal legs. I've lived long enough to see gods born and die, but damned if I always get the jimmy legs after astral travel. It's such a bother. Give me a moment."

The two unmoving forms on the bed waited patiently, blood trickling to the bed through hundreds of holes drilled through their flesh.

"I've got it. I've got it. Oh, no I don't—" the voice cut off with a crash.

THE DARK BROWN OXFORD loafer lowered and came to rest on the floor...and set down on the root-strewn floor with no issues. Presently, a well-dressed man followed the loafer, looking very pleased for some reason and looking around as if he were awaiting praise.

When none came, his lips pressed into a thin line. Eyes that have seen eons, have seen the birth and death of entire galaxies, strafed around the room, and where his gaze fell, reality itself shivered. Finally, after taking in the room and the beautiful destruction his roots had wrought, he turned to the bed where he expected to see two immobile forms riddled with his blood red tendrils.

"What—"

A loud, shuddering moan interrupted his question. The young man and lady who had made his traversal of the universe possible, the young man and woman who *should* be mere husks of brittle bones and desiccated flesh, writhed on the bed, rutting like the end times were upon them. The dapper gentleman's eyes widened in shock. While he watched, the virile young man repositioned so he knelt behind the young lady, herself on hands and knees like a wild animal.

Animals were exactly what they sounded like, as well, as Sam began to piston his hips like a locomotive.

"I say... I say, stop that. Stop that at once."

Sam swept a strand of sweaty hair from his face and met the gentleman's eyes...and grinned. For the first time, the gentleman noticed that their bodies, while doused in sweat and no doubt other bodily fluids, were whole and hale.

"You're supposed to be dead!"

Sam's grin widened. "Hexazinone," he said, and his rhythm never faltered. With obvious glee, Sam issued a hearty slap to the lady's posterior.

The gentleman felt his face flush, which shouldn't even be possible—blasted mortal flesh!—and he averted his eyes. With willpower that had enslaved millions, he returned his attention to the young man. "*Explain*," he commanded through gritted teeth, and he hated himself for the emotion tinging his words.

Sam jerked his head and it took a moment for the gentleman to realize the young man was trying to draw his attention to a line that ringed the bed on the floor. "Hexazinone," he said again. "It's a powder herbicide. Among other things, it kills tree roots."

Understanding dawned, and he gasped. "It—it kills..." His mouth flapped and words failed him. "Now, see here, mortal. I've traveled farther than your puny mind can comprehend—"

"***No***." The scorn, the conviction, the power, behind the word made even the gentleman pull up short. "*You* listen. I've been in love with this girl since I was five years old. There's nothing in the universe I'm going to let come between us."

Disgust curled the gentleman's lip. "You filthy, rutting—"

"*Enough*." This time is was the young lady who spoke, and the word cracked through the room like a whip. But her gaze wasn't even on him. It was like he didn't even exist. She gyrated her hips, causing Sam to close his eyes and moan. "Less talk, more action."

Sam shrugged at the gentleman—as if to say *what can ya do?*—then issued another slap to Ash's posterior and returned his attention to her fully. It was a long, long time before they realized the gentleman, and the hole to the other side of the universe, had both disappeared.

THE ACCURSED

"Let me see."

Ash lifted the old painting fully out of the cardboard box and handed it to Judy. The proprietor of Heavenly Treasures took it, her hands dipping from the surprising weight of it. The ancient wood grain scraped against her calloused hands as she turned the painting around so she could study it. After a few moments, her brow furrowed.

"What's wrong?" Ash asked.

"I know what this is."

"Ancient porn..." Sam spoke under his breath, but not so low that Ash couldn't hear it. Without looking, she jabbed an elbow into his rips. He yelped in surprise, then fell into a sullen silence, rubbing at the sore spot.

"What is it?" Excitement tinged Ash's voice. Years of thrifting with her mom and Alice Dyer had instilled a deep-grained thirst for finding hidden gems. Judy turned a solemn expression on Ash, and Ash's excitement redoubled. She was practically vibrating with it.

"Evil."

"Wait, what?" The excitement leaked out of her like air from a popped balloon.

"This painting," Judy said, brandishing it as if the two of them didn't know which painting she was talking about. "It's evil."

"It's... Hold on, Judy. I don't—I don't understand."

Sensing that his friend was going to be tongue tied for a while, Sam jumped in. "How can a painting be evil?"

"Haven't you two ever seen a scary movie? Read a horror novel?" At their blank expressions, she continued. "There's always some kind of evil McGuffin. A cursed artifact, demon necklace, or something.

Ridiculous trope if you ask me, but what can you do. That's what this is."

Ash finally found her tongue. "Don't be silly. If you don't like it, I'd be happy to buy it."

"Oh no, girlie. Not on your life. This thing is going in the incinerator."

"You have an incinerator?"

Ash thought Sam sounded way too excited about this development, but she ignored him and pressed on. "Okay, Judy. Joke's over. How much for the painting?"

Instead of answering, Judy turned and disappeared into the storeroom. Ash and Sam trailed behind her, through a door Ash had never noticed before and down a dark set of stairs. At the bottom, a line of footprints through the dust marked Judy's path across the room. A black iron monstrosity, something that looked straight out of Nightmare on Elm Street, sat in the corner, a dizzying spiderweb of pipes shooting from its bulbous form.

"Is anyone else really horny all of a sudden?"

Dim, watery light streamed through the doorway above, but it was still enough for Ash to see Sam leaning forward to check out the prodigious bulge in his own jeans. She was intrigued, but wrenched her attention back to Judy. The door to the furnace screeched on rusted hinges and a gust of heat blasted over them.

She's serious, Ash thought with a pang of realization. *The old gal has gone batty.*

The ornate frame was too large to fit through the door straight on. Even turned diagonal, Judy had to manhandle it into the blazing furnace.

THE ACCURSED

Out of nowhere, an otherwordly voice echoed through the room, like it was coming from a distant tunnel. Strangely, it had a British accent.

"Unhand me, you daft crone! This isn't how it's supposed to—"

There was a sharp, splintering snap, and with one last heave, Judy thrust the painting into the fire.

The heavy iron door muffled the disembodied voice. "Hello? Can you hear me? Is this thing still work—"

The End

THE SWEAT HAD FINALLY evaporated from their bodies but the sheets under them were still damp. Every time they moved she caught another whiff of the musky scent of sweat and sex. Thirty minutes ago the air had still been laden with it, but it had finally dissipated.

Ash forcibly pushed aside the thoughts that bubbled up and turned the last page, resting her hand on the stack of papers. "Well...that's it."

Now that they weren't reading together, Sam shifted to make a little space between them. "I still don't get it."

"What?"

"The title."

"What's to get? It's called *The Curse*."

"No, not that. Eldritch Affair. Were you supposed to fuck the guy in the suit or something?" He threw up his hands in mock surrender when Ash turned a glare his way. "What? It's called '*affair*'."

Her sharp gaze softened. A bit. "Not that kind of affair. I think it means affair as in... a something."

"A something?"

She slapped his chest. "Shut up. *You're* the nerd, not me. Affair as in...a proceeding or event or..."

"Something," Sam provided. She glared at him again and he kissed her to indicate his surrender. "Okay, but what about the author's name?"

"What about it?"

"Is it really supposed to fool anyone?"

"What do you mean?" She shifted toward him, laying her head on him. Absently, her fingers played with the wispy hair on his chest and stomach.

"Riain Fox. It sounds like Ryan Fox. You know, exactly like the other author. Are we really supposed to believe it's a different person?"

"It's pronounce Riain, not Ryan."

"You just said the same thing."

Ash dug her nails into his side to show her displeasure. Sam laughed and bucked, and because he was still naked and her head was on his stomach, she almost got a face full. He laughed again.

"Careful, or I'm going to dig my nails into somewhere much more tender."

"Promises, promises."

She narrowed her eyes and glared at him, her hand inching down his body. "*Anyways...* It's not supposed to fool anyone. It's a pen name. For marketing, so Riain's readers know that Ryan's books are a different genre."

"So *Ryan*'s readers know that *Ryan's* books are a different genre?" He grinned...until Ash's hand slipped down lower and she made good on her promise.

About the Author

Riain Fox is the pen name for author Ryan W. Fox and his wife. Together, they write sexy, scary stories. They live in Northern California with their two children and a growing menagerie of pets.

To keep up to date, join the mailing list, or get in touch check out ryanwfox.com.

The Trouble with Typos

Despite many, many rounds of editing, typos and errors sometimes slip through. If you find any errors, please let me know. You can email me at riain@prometheanbooks.com

Thank you!

Made in the USA
Las Vegas, NV
11 August 2023